BAQWA PRESENTS: TOGETHER

BAY AREA QUEER WRITERS ASSOCIATION
ANTHOLOGY VOLUME 4

K.S. TRENTEN ● PAT HENSHAW

R.L. MERRILL ● LIZ FARAIM

RICHARD MAY ● VINCENT TRAUGHBER MEIS

M.D. NEU ● WAYNE GOODMAN

MICHAEL ALENYIKOV ● SARAH WHITE

RICH RUBIN ● JAN STECKEL

ISBN: 978-1-959257-09-7

Copyright © 2024

Design/Layout: Wayne Goodman

waynegoodmanbooks

waynegoodmanbooks@gmail.com
Twitter: @WGoodmanbooks

Print versions at independent booksellers
Electronic versions on Kindle and Nook
Audiobooks from Audible and iTunes

About BAQWA

The Bay Area Queer Writers Association is a group of local writers who support and encourage each other.

The goal of the group is to create a strong visible writing community here in the San Francisco Bay Area. They are based in Silicon Valley, but they have members from all over the Bay Area.

This group is open to anyone who loves to read and wants to help support area authors. You don't have to live in the Bay Area to be a member, you just have to love Queer books and enjoy reading.

For more information, please visit https://baqwawriters.wixsite.com/books

TABLE OF CONTENTS

Together

K.S. Trenten

We walk hand in hand
  Together
We shiver in the cold
  Together
Sweat sticks to our restless fingers
All of this this brings us
  Together.

We don't need to say a word
  Together
We enjoy the silence, the kiss of the breeze
  Together.

A screech of tires comes at us
The rattle of a child, racing on a metal contraption
We swallow our panic, aware we are vulnerable
  Together.

We see a thousand smiles
We face a thousand scowls
We hold our heads up high
Radiating pride
  Together.

We're divided by a mass of clutter
We argue over frivolities
We walk in separate directions
We are no longer
  Together.

We sleep alone
No longer sharing a worn blanket
I marvel at how cold it is
Making me all the more aware
We are no longer
  Together.

We walk hand in hand
  Together

I walk alone in silence with my thoughts
Aware of the empty spaces
The smiles and scowls are harder to bear
Harder than when we were
   Together.

I bump into you walking
Looking rather lost
We start to smile, only to look away
How awkward we've become
Now that we're no longer
   Together.

I ask if you'd like to walk with me
You start, only to start smiling
I realize how much I've missed your face
A face I used to see everyday
Back when we were
   Together.

We start to walk, side by side
Daring to enjoy each other's company
Everything still lies between us
This moment is enough
Now that we are once again
   Together.

Bon Appetit:
A Love Story Amid Food

Pat Henshaw

*You learn a lot about someone when you share a meal together. – **Anthony Bourdain***

First Course: Hors d'oeuvres

"Happy big birthday! Welcome to the Land of the Under-appreciated and Love Hungry."

"Speak for yourself, Marco Polo. May I be the first to say, I look good at thirty. But you? Merely a husk of a man, dried up and bitter, floating out in the world hoping to latch onto something. Or is it someone?"

Peter Lamont and Mark Trainor hugged, a full-body clasp which shouted it had been too long since they last got together, even though it had only been a few weeks. Peter had turned thirty in March, but today promised a gorgeous sunset in June for Mark's slip down the slide of youth.

"So, what is this place now?" Mark looked around at the changes to the pier. Restaurants, stalls, shops, and a huge arcade had popped up on the widened, safer jetty.

"Tonight's an experiment. I thought it would be fun to celebrate your coming-of-old-age with a progressive meal." Peter gave a game show host wave of his hand. "We're eating the first course here at Mama Mia's and then traveling to other establishments for each part of a traditional five course meal. There might be a surprise at the end. It is your birthday, after all."

Mark sat in the chair Peter indicated. It was early for dinner, so they were one of only a few couples.

"Ah. So, do we order? Look at a menu? Or just wait for –" Mark's words halted as a waiter put a tray of hors d'oeuvres on the table with a demi-bottle of wine and two glasses.

The waiter uncorked, poured, and gave the tasting glass to Peter. After his nod and Mark's glass was filled, they were left to the tray of goodies.

Mark picked up a tiny piece of toast with something beige smeared on it, a slice of black olive and sliver of pimento decorated it. Before he put it into his mouth, he studied it.

"This kinda reminds me of the refreshments when we met." He popped it in his mouth, chewed, swallowed, and smacked his lips. "Tastes better, though."

"I should hope so." Peter laughed. "Why I ever thought going to a Speed Dating for Gays was a good idea is beyond me. And we were both freshmen. Barely nineteen. Good thing I met you or it would have been a total loss."

They shared a fond smile, their eyes sparkling in agreement.

"God, what a disaster of an evening." Mark ate a piece of ham rolled around something white and followed it with a mushroom cap stuffed with what looked like piped cheese and topped with a slice of almond. He licked his fingers. "Remember the older man, the returning student? He'd seen the posters around campus and thought it would be a bunch of night school students like him."

They both chuckled at the memory.

"Yeah, he looked like our chaperone. We could have all been his grandchildren."

"Or great-grandchildren," Mark agreed. "Yeah, I felt sorry for him and for the three lesbians since everyone else was male."

"Yeah, they should have left right away and gone to have coffee in the student café. At least they wouldn't have had to answer the organizer's stupid questions and act like they were interested in seeing any of the rest of us ever again."

Mark grunted in agreement. He'd been eating steadily through the small plate of canapes.

"The saving grace of the evening came when this incredibly handsome pre-law student walked in and sat down at my table." Peter put his hand on Mark's arm for a second. "He'd just found out his lover was a cheat and liar. He had a broken heart and a very, very bad attitude about love and dating. I didn't know why he stuck around."

Mark nodded and wiped his fingers and lips with his napkin. His long, thin fingers matched his graceful dancer build. In the courtroom, his actions were smooth and reassuring as much as his words were hard-hitting and decisive. With his dark hair and blazing eyes, he looked like an avenger, not a rumpled lawyer.

"I don't know about the handsome bit," he answered Peter, "but I do know I was looking for a fight and some rough I-can-cheat-too sex. Being so young, I really believed both would make me feel better. Besides, I'd promised one of the organizers I'd show up. He would have haunted me if I hadn't." Mark shook his head. "Then I sat down at the table of an angel and found out I was wrong to be reluctant to be there. Participating in the speed date and then having you pick me up and coerce me to go for coffee were soul cleansing. We laughed at and mocked my ex and the event for hours."

Peter grabbed the last of the hors d'oeuvres. He swiped his brown-blond mix of hair off his forehead, but the wind swept it back. Peter looked like everyone's favorite neighborhood kid. He might seem to be part imp and part scamp, but he was always reliable, polite, and caring. He was a wonderful barnacle who latched onto someone and made their life happier.

Mark sighed. "I would have done something really stupid that night if it hadn't been for you."

Peter erupted with a little giggle. "Oh, I would have loved to have seen you fight. You! Fighting! Oh, my."

"Hey, hey. I can hold my own if I have to." Mark's hands formed fists, and he shook them at Peter.

Peter smiled at the silliness of the gesture and checked his watch.

"Eat up. We're on a time schedule of sorts." He stood and waved at the waiter. "We're off. The food was delicious. You can report back to Mama I'm telling everyone at work about this place."

The waiter nodded and scurried off to help someone else.

Mark looked a little stunned but got up and followed Peter.

"You know what sticks in my mind the most from then?"

Peter turned and took Mark's hand.

"What?"

Mark looked down at their hands.

"You hugged me and touched me constantly. I didn't know how much I needed it."

Peter squeezed his hand. Mark sighed. He turned to Peter and pulling him close, hugged him. Peter smiled to himself and hugged Mark back. He knew how much his friend needed to be touched.

"Thank you," Mark murmured.

"No, thank you. You saved me as much as I helped you. I was lost on campus and needed a friend. Someone I could laugh and joke with. Someone who wanted sex as much as I did."

With a laugh, he gave Mark one last hug.

"Now let's get some more to eat."

Second Course: Soup

"Our second journey back in time leads to the Good Samaritan Shelter." Peter gestured to Soup It Up Café as Mark groaned.

While a waiter wearing an apron with an oversized logo seated them, they looked around at the country kitchen themed space with red-and-white-checkered tablecloths, pottery dinnerware, recycled wood walls, and dried herbs hanging in bundles over them. The place was much busier than Mama Mia's. Although the décor wasn't like Good Samaritan's, the crowded tables and jostling crowd were. Unlike Good Samaritan's these diners weren't smelly men and occasional women off the streets who stood in line to eat each evening. This place reeked of family.

"Hey, I was going through my do-gooder phase," Mark protested. "Because of you, I might add."

"Your grudging, complaining, growling do-gooder moment I think you mean," Peter added. "You showed up, what? Three times. The first time after a day of drinking when you could barely stand and called me to come bail you out."

Even though Soup It Up wanted to be an upscale café, the noise level screamed big, vocal family at the holidays. There might have been ambient music, but no one could hear it.

"Hey, my bad mood and drinking were all your fault. I'd been to see the shrink you forced me to visit that morning. A shrink who 'drilled down' into my unhappiness at getting dumped a second time by the scumbag boyfriend. I was drowning my sorrows, including my shitty taste in men and my incredible stupidity in thinking a man who once cheated on me wouldn't actually do it again." Mark grimaced. "I know, I know. You warned me. And I got mad at you. Sorry to have been such a loser friend."

Peter held up his hands in a defensive gesture as they were served the soup of the day. The herbs hanging from the hooks overhead might be decoration, but by the delicious smell, they could tell the chef used them well in his creations.

"Not a loser. Eternally hopeful. Eat up. This looks delicious."

Both men tucked in as if they hadn't just eaten a few moments before.

"I might remind you, you agreed to see the shrink, Mark. And, you did say you felt better for having gone." Then Peter grinned, his trademark dimples and twinkly eyes making Mark feel better, as usual. "Well, at least you said you felt better after I came to your rescue at the soup kitchen. You even said the experience with your ex and with the shrink had made you a better man. So, you decided to help out on the serving line at the shelter."

Mark sighed. "Yeah, okay, I know you think I'm a quitter and a loser." He held up a hand to stop Peter from speaking. "Not your turn to talk, okay?"

At Peter's nod, Mark continued.

"I just hadn't found the right way to help others. My way to help. Standing in a serving line and watching man after man walk by getting a bowl of soup, roll, butter, and drink didn't make me feel like I was really helping. All it did was remind me over and over that *there but for the grace of God go I*."

They ate in silence for a few minutes.

"My turn to talk now?" Peter asked.

Mark dunked his roll into the broth. "Yeah, I guess." He sounded sullen and resentful.

"I understood. Then and now. Your grandfather had just died. Your boyfriend cheated—again. You were starting law school. The world was coming down around you. I got it—I get it. Then you volunteered in good faith to help at the soup kitchen..."

"Because you said I needed to get out of myself!"

"And that's why I wasn't a very good friend..."

"No, you've always been my best friend. Always. You were right, but not at the time. I needed other advice. I just needed..." Mark sighed. "I just needed more hugs and someone to hold me at night and to tell me things would get better. That's what I really needed, and you gave them to me. Again."

He started to scoop up the last of his soup but dropped his spoon in the bowl.

"Dammit! Every time we get together, I promise not to get like this—all touchy-feely, and replaying the past." He stared at Peter. "It's time we moved on. Look to the future. You know, think positive. Not wade through the past again."

Peter grinned at him.

"Good idea. What better way to celebrate a monumental birthday? Off with the old. On with the new. You got any ideas of how you want things to change?"

The waiter was hovering, and Peter realized they were supposed to be on their way. He also mentally slapped himself for bringing up Good Samaritan. Not the mood he wanted to set tonight. Not at all.

Third Course: Salad

Garden of Eden looked like a greenhouse that had lost its way on a pier with the ocean churning on all sides beneath the newly-installed walkway.

Mark stopped at the entrance, and Peter gave him a tiny shove to move him inside.

"I know you hate salads," Peter whispered in Mark's ear. "But a traditional five course meal includes one. I would never skip a course on your birthday."

Mark grimaced and set his shoulders. "Into the breach!"

"That's the spirit," Peter said with a chuckle. "Buck up, buttercup. Don't worry. We won't stay long."

"I think we're burning up more calories than we're taking in tonight. And this stop won't add any more."

"Don't worry. There's more to come." Peter nudged him gently as they followed the waiter to their table.

Once Peter showed his vouchers, the mixed greens, bowl of salad veggies, and tray of dressing choices appeared immediately.

"See? It's create your own salad. You can have most of the veg and none of the greens if you'd like." Peter passed him the bowl of raw vegetables.

"Huh." Mark scooped them into his low bowl as Peter lined his with greens. "This isn't such a bad idea."

"Knew you'd like it. Now you were saying about changes?"

Mark picked up his fork, speared a baby tomato, and ate it. He shook his head.

"Let's finish this first," he said. "I'd rather talk about the future over some real food than over this rabbit fare."

Peter choked on a laugh.

"Yeah. Okay. Fine."

They ate quickly, each eager to get on with the meal, but more importantly with their plans for the years to come.

Fourth Course: Main

Peter knew Chow Down would be Mark's favorite of the moveable feast. The specialties of meat and potatoes were featured alongside the more prevalent refillable seafood baskets. This was not the place for vegetarians, vegans, or other save-the-planet diners. Peter expected a room full of huge bellicose men brandishing steak knives and cutting into bleeding meat platters.

Instead, he saw a handful of average mixed and same-sex couples, people he would see every day walking around neighborhoods at work.

Mark took one huge breath and sighed.

"Food!" he murmured and followed the waiter to their table.

After telling him how he wanted his porterhouse cooked, Mark grinned at Peter.

"Thank you! I know it was a temptation to skip this red meat stop, but I appreciate your agreeing to pander to my inner caveman." Mark took a swig of the local microbrew and smacked his lips. "Yup. Tastes great. We've got time to have a few more beers, right?"

Peter nodded and sipped his water. He had already decided he was the designated driver.

The food arrived quicker than Peter expected. They hadn't even had time to start the serious discussion.

"So, you were talking about the future?" Peter ate some of his salmon and wild rice.

"Yeah. Let me start at last month." Mark wiped his mouth and drank some water. "I was at this party one of the younger guys at the firm had thrown. You know the kind where you drop by and stay as long as you like. And no one pays attention to the coming and going. Everyone drinking, the vibe slow and seductive, the natives sniffing around for the lay of the night. Mostly queer but some others. You know."

Peter nodded. They'd both slowed their eating, both intent on what Mark was saying.

"I'd been annoyed with the day when I'd first walked in the front door. Then one of the interns slid by me and muttered, 'Daddy, come find me later.'"

Peter gasped. "Daddy!?"

"Yup. Shocking the first time, but even worse as I heard it over and over. *Daddy?* Me? Hell, no. I'm still young. I was still young. I'm still young, aren't I?" Mark picked up his glass, stared at its contents, sighed, and put it back down on the table.

"I sat on a couch that was pushed up against the wall and watched the guys at the party. Every kind of gay guy and queer you could ever want, all parading back and forth, trying so hard to be picked. They didn't have to scream, 'Me! Me! Fuck me!' because their clothes, makeup, strutting, hand gestures, everything about them was a calculated arrow pointing at their real or imagined assets.

"I sat on the lush purple velvet couch in my beige chinos, Vans, and Izod shirt. No makeup, no glitz, no glamor, just me... and what my family calls my brilliant mind. Not one damn person in the room cared about sitting down and talking to me about something other than my yearly salary. I would have even talked about the weather or sports. But, no, no one. The few who stopped by to chat only cared how much money 'Daddy' made. I could hear their minds wondering how much of it they could have IF they could put up with 'Daddy' long enough.

"I was amazed–and tried to be amused–by how quickly I can bore people. My people. I realized I'd wasted so much time at parties like this when I could have been..."

Mark sighed.

Peter's head was down. His face reflected his dismay.

"First off, you're not boring," he started.

"Hush. It's my turn to talk. I walked out of the party, having interacted meaningfully with no one. I came home, drank a glass of ice water, and planted myself on the sofa. Then a weird kind of panic started to settle in.

"Where was I going? What was I doing to make myself happy? In five, ten, twenty-five years, would I still be sitting here feeling absolutely nothing, filling my days with work and conferences? Only seeing you when we're both available?"

Mark looked up at Peter who was now staring at him with a slight smile on his lips. Peter's hand clasped his.

"Don't worry. I have a solution. A solution I think you'll really, really like."

Peter grinned. Mark's mouth slowly mimicked his.

When their waiter cleared his throat in a blatant reminder they needed to move on, Peter said, "Hold that thought, Mark. We need to be at our next stop."

Dutifully, Mark followed Peter as they made their way to the Sweet Stop.

Fifth Course: Dessert

The beautiful sunset had vanished, blown away by the swirling fog around the pier. Instead of the blazing glory of romance lingering in the sky, the landscape now spoke of gentle, intimate words whispered in a lover's ear, as when a couple walked along the beach back home.

"Hey! You guys got here. I was wondering if your order would melt before you came in. Frosting doesn't do well in heavy mist or fog." The waiter gave a worried smile. "Right this way. Follow me."

They were led to a window table overlooking the swirling fog as it danced up to glance at them before it flitted away.

After they were seated, the waiter said, "I'll be right back with your dessert!" He turned and walked quickly back to the serving counter.

"Before he gets back, I have to finish my story." Mark stood and got down on one knee next to Peter, who gasped.

"I love you. I've always loved you. I never wanted to be fuck buddies or whatever we've been for years. I may be a hotshot in court, but I could never find the words to say this. I. Love. You. I want to spend my life with you. I'll change jobs. I'll relocate to L.A. I'll do anything so we can be together. I love you."

Mark was practically crying.

"Hey, hey. It's okay. It's all right." Peter bent over to kiss Mark as the waiter put down a tray of four cupcakes with burning birthday candles on them. "Why don't you blow out your candles and make your birthday wish and then we'll talk?"

Peter helped Mark stand and turned him toward the cupcakes. Without really focusing on them, Mark blew out the candles and then looked down.

Four cupcakes piled high with frosting held the smoldering candles and four notecards on toothpicks. The cards read:

♥ WILL
♥ YOU
♥ MARRY
♥ ME

Je vous aime.
Laissez le bon temps rouler!

SOLD AS IS

R.L. MERRILL

Was it a misunderstanding,
Or an intentional slight,
That brought me to the
Dead end street that night?

I checked and rechecked
The numbers and spelling
On the back of the business card
That led me to the dwelling.

Darkness clung to the structure
I'd been hired to sell.
It was described "a fixer-upper"
They left out a "dungeon of hell."

I stepped out of the car
And looked around the cul-de-sac.
The house stood alone,
As though neighbors were taken aback.

By the light of the moon and
One solitary streetlight,
I beheld what was once a jewel
But now a neglected blight.

It was a shame to see
This once magnificent place,
Left in such a state
When previously it held such grace.

I took in a breath
And reached out with my senses,
Beyond the overgrown vines
Covering the iron fences.

"Show me your beauty,"
I whispered into the night.
I smelled rotting wood
And stagnant water out of sight.

Mixed with the blood
Of a forgotten murder,
The living memory of which
Marked me an intruder.

"Show me your splendor
As it once was beheld."
With a furtive glance, I drew on
Past and present to meld.

An image of the house
On a bright spring day
With a manicured yard
And white paint trimmed in gray.

I held the vision
In the front of my mind,
To attempt to manifest
And the image to bind.

A blur caught my eye
As I worked the spell.
A hand brushed my neck
Where my short blonde bob fell.

I gasped and turned sharply
To look at the porch
Where a figure was standing
Their glow bright as a torch.

"Excuse me," I called out.
"I'm here from Magic Realty."
The figure stepped forward
Presenting a woman quite pretty.

"It's a beautiful home underneath,"
I said with a gesture about.
She took in my measure
Her expression full of doubt.

"I can perform a makeover.
You might've heard I'm a whiz."
She shook her head slowly.
"It must be sold as is."

The vision of her was translucent.
The darkness blurred her edges.
She appeared to hover
Above the unkempt hedges.

"The house must be sold as is,"
She repeated in a distorted voice.
She rested a hand on the column
As she stood with such poise.

Warmth flooded me
As I stared at her face,
Her rounded belly and ample hips,
The way she commanded the space.

I was drawn to her,
Her words seemed a warning.
I ignored the morsel of fear,
Not afraid she'd scorn me.

For I sensed that behind
Her vengeful guise
Was loneliness
And fear, I surmised.

"Let me come in
And show you my plans.
I'll respect your wishes
and meet your demands."

I concentrated on making
The steps solid under my feet
As I approached her on the porch
Glad my appearance was neat.

I didn't recognize her
Or the place's violent history.
To me she was lovely,
The house, an enticing mystery.

She reached out to touch
A lock of my hair
And I felt her movement
Disturb the air.

A shiver ran through me
Clear out to my fingers.
I wanted to touch her,
Caress her, and linger.

"It must be sold as is,"
She whispered in my ear.
Her ghostly hand gripped my neck
But strangely, I had no fear.

Her gaze moved suddenly
to the path through the garden.
I turned to find my boss.
"What are you doing here, Martin?"

His features were pulled
Into an angry grimace
"I should ask what you
are doing on these premises."

"Found a card with this old listing
And thought I could assist
With a bit of a makeover."
The apparition grabbed my wrist.

"You shouldn't have come,"
He said coming closer.
She pulled me back.
"Sold as is," she whispered.

I was blinded by a flash,
A series of brutal images,
Of Martin and the woman,
Her death shown in stages.

First, he smiled brightly
As he offered his services.
When she refused
They awakened his urges.

There was a struggle.
There were screams.
There ran blood,
In crimson streams.

She fought his advances
But he was stronger.
The scene was torture.
I could watch no longer.

"Leave this place,"
I growled at my boss.
"I cannot do that, and
You know why *Miz* Ross."

"You won't get away with it."
Though I knew he likely would.
I'd try to stop him.
I'd fight as hard as I could.

But my magic was for creation
And though it was strong,
It didn't work for protection.
I couldn't hold him off long.

But I had an idea,
One last-ditch attempt.
I conjured up matter
As strong as cement.

It swirled around his feet
Where he stood ready to attack
The mass crept up his legs
And over his back.

"This is for all of us
You tried to silence.
This prison will hold you
And protect us from violence."

I focused on molding
The matter to his body.
He renewed his pleas
But he couldn't stop me.

The thick covering immobilized him,
Inch by inch,
And when it reached its face,
His cries cut off with a pinch.

I turned to find the woman
Smiling in relief,
"You have a new statue."
It fell like a leaf.

I gave it a push
And one last shove.
She descended the steps
An angel from above.

Gone was my supervisor,
The lord of crass
Who fondled and groped
Every woman's ass.

I sighed with relief
No longer in his employ
"Come inside,"
The ghost spoke with joy.

"Let's talk of your plans,"
She said with a smile.
"And maybe then,
You can stay awhile."

I liked her suggestion.
I straightened my blouse
And without another question,
Followed her into the house.

On Samhain it's said,
The veil becomes thin
And specters may warn you
Of evil and sin.

Do not be afraid,
If you are of good heart.
For magic will protect you
And a new love may start.

BULLSEYE

LIZ FARAIM

Nervous energy coursed through me as I pulled into the gravel lot of the shooting range. The range property was massive and contained several specialty shooting areas. I'd gotten turned around a few times trying to find the exact place I was supposed to be, costing me precious minutes.

There were no shaded parking spots to be had, so I pulled into the first empty space I found and threw my Jeep into park. Stepping out, my boots crunched in the gravel and, despite it being just after sunrise, the day was already warming up. I hurriedly collected my range bag and pistol case and strode down a driveway toward the shooting bays. The red range flag was down, and the air silent, so I didn't need my earmuffs yet.

A man in matching red range master T-shirt and ball cap stood near the bottom of the hill. He appeared to be waiting for new and disoriented people like me, to help guide us.

"Good morning. I'm here for the defensive accuracy class."

"Mornin'. Head on down to bay one." He motioned to his left, past a metal-sided building.

"Thanks."

I strode past the building, its side already radiating heat, and reminded myself to stand up straight. Walking into firearms classes without knowing anyone was always daunting. Not because I was a bad shot—in fact I was a kick ass shot—but because I was almost always the only woman, and the men were usually ultra conservative while I was an obviously butch lesbian. I stood out.

Drawing in a deep breath, I smelled eucalyptus in the air, which helped steady me. Striding confidently around the corner of the building, our workspace for the day lay before me. There were ten men lined up at a dusty worktop. Camp chairs were arranged haphazardly under a large shade tent, and someone had set up a misting fan which was already on full blast.

I chastised myself for not having left the house fifteen minutes earlier. Being one of the last people to arrive was embarrassing. The men had already spread out their stuff, taking up the entire worktop. Putting on a smile and straightening my shoulders, I approached.

"Good morning, gents. Mind if I squeeze in here?"

Some looked up from their tasks. For a moment, no one moved. They all seemed satisfied with the tabletop spaces they had claimed and hesitant to give them up.

A man standing at the head of the table relented, giving me a welcoming smile, and scooted his stuff over to make room. "Howdy. Come on down. There's plenty of room, right guys?"

Several of the men mumbled in agreement and looked away.

"Thanks." I placed my range bag down on the tabletop. "Name's Dusty. You?"

I extended my hand, and he shook it heartily, his muddy brown eyes gleaming.

"Nice to meet ya, Dusty. I'm Frank. Happy to share a spot with you. We're just loading up our magazines. Uh... you know what a magazine is, dontcha? I know sometimes they call them clips on the TV, but magazine is the correct term."

Biting back the profanity that wanted to come out of my mouth, I smiled at Frank again.

"Yes, I do know what a magazine is. I believe it could be described as a spring-powered ammunition storage and feeding device that, once loaded, is inserted into our semi-automatic pistols. This isn't an entry level class, Frank."

"Well crap. Sounds to me like you could write the book on pistols. I'll bite my tongue."

I gave him a nod and unzipped my range bag, pulling empty magazines from one pocket and a large box of 9mm ammunition from another.

Loading the pistol magazines with ammunition, I enjoyed the sensation of pressing smooth metal rounds against the tight springs inside the magazine. I counted each round I loaded so I wouldn't come up short.

A murmur ran through the group. I paused the count in my head and looked toward the walkway. Someone loaded up with shooting gear rounded the corner of the warehouse. I quickly registered she was a woman. She wore a close-fitting white shirt emblazoned with various competitive shooting logos, and had a perky ponytail poking out the back of her ball cap. She had on some highly technical pants that hugged her body.

I turned to Frank. "It appears our final student has arrived. The dirty dozen is complete."

He nodded, grinning. I cleared my throat.

"Good morning. Come on down. We'll clear a spot for you." I looked to the man next to me. "Right?"

He gave me a nod and consolidated his gear, making room for her. She strode confidently over, her ponytail swinging, and placed her bag next to mine. I offered her my hand. She shook it, her slim smooth fingers strong against mine.

"Dusty."

"Nao."

"Now?"

She chuckled. "No, Nao. It's Japanese."

A hot blush rose up my neck as I realized my mistake.

"Ah, I see. Well, Nao, it's nice to meet you."

"Likewise."

She opened her range bag, and I returned to loading ammunition, one round at a time, counting along in my head. My count was interrupted by a rapid clacking sound next to me. Nao had used a speed loader and pushed ten rounds into her first magazine in a matter of seconds.

"Well, heck. Now, that's the way to get it done. Nice." Frank said, looking at her speed loader in wonder.

"It works for me," she said flippantly.

Two more quick rounds with the speed loader and she was finished. She wandered off to find a spot for her camp chair while Frank and I finished hand loading our rounds.

Frank leaned in conspiratorially. "Something tells me she could teach this class."

"You're probably right."

I joined Nao in a slim line of shade she had found against the wall of the building, quickly unfolding my camp chair and placing it next to hers.

"Did you happen to see the forecasted high for today, Dusty?"

"I did. One hundred and four degrees by this afternoon, they say."

She scoffed and pulled on a pair of sun sleeves to protect the skin of her arms. I stood and stepped away, applying sunscreen spray to my arms, neck, and face. The scent of synthetic coconuts filled the air. I detested the way the oily layer felt on my skin but knew it was necessary. Maybe she was onto something by wearing her high-tech sun sleeves. I held the bottle of sunblock out toward her.

"Like to have some for your face or neck?"

"No, I'm all set. Thanks."

I wiped my palms along the front of my tactical pants, trying to get the oily sunblock off. It doesn't take a genius to know it is not wise to handle a pistol with a slick grip.

John clapped his hands to get the group's attention. "Circle up, folks. Let's get started."

Nao and I took our places among the other students standing in the middle of the shooting bay. A small breeze blew a puff of dust from the ground. Five men, all wearing the same red range officer hats and shirts, stood shoulder to shoulder in front of us.

"Good morning. You should all be here for defensive accuracy training. If you haven't already signed in on the clipboard, please do so after this briefing. I'm John, the Chief Range Officer for today. These other fellas, Brian, Bryan, Kai, and Chuck will be your instructors. We have a long day ahead of us. It is imperative that you stay hydrated and follow all the safety guidelines. Any serious violations will get you sent home immediately. Are we all in agreement that nobody wants to leave here today with any new holes in their body?"

The group chuckled nervously.

"I'm serious. Do you want a new hole in your body today?"

It took a moment before I realized he was pointing a thick finger at me. Nao gave me a slight nudge.

Tersely, I responded. "No, sir. I do not."

"All right. Now, if there is an accidental discharge today that results in a bullet wound, one of the instructors will call 9-1-1. Do NOT call 9-1-1 and tell them someone has been shot. If you do that, they send the police first and make the ambulance wait, which delays crucial medical care. People can bleed out in a matter of minutes. For 9-1-1, we call it a 'training accident.' Everyone got it?"

The group seemed to collectively wake up and all responded with a resounding "Yes."

"Good. Now, let's talk safety..."

The first half of the day flew by as we moved through various shooting scenarios. It wasn't until lunch break that I realized I had sweat through my shirt and was dizzy despite having guzzled water during each break.

I sat heavily in my camp chair, setting my small ice chest on my lap. The small strip of shade our chairs had been in had grown, and Nao and I had a nice shady corner to ourselves. I unzipped the lid of my ice chest and frowned. The peanut butter and honey sandwich, string cheese, and banana did nothing to inspire my appetite.

Nao pulled several glass food containers from her ice chest, which caught my attention.

"What have you got there?"

"Green salad, some cubed watermelon, and onigiri."

"Onigiri? May I ask what that is?"

"Rice balls. Good for when I am on the go. What about you?"

"Just boring stuff. Sandwich, cheese stick, banana."

She raised her eyebrows, giving me a smile. "That sounds... uh..."

"Boring? It is."

I took a bite of my sandwich, reminding myself to be grateful.

"Would you like to try a rice ball?"

"I don't want to take your lunch."

"It's no trouble. It's just one. I'm happy to share."

"All right."

I extended a hand to her, grimacing at the stains deep in the creases of my hand and the grit under my fingernails. I had scrubbed my hands with pumice soap before sitting down to eat, but they were permanently stained from work.

She placed an onigiri in my hand. It was rice shaped like a triangle and had what appeared to be seaweed wrapped around half of it. I gave her a nod and pushed the entire thing into my mouth. The salty seasoning played across my tongue, and the rice was the perfect texture as I chewed. I hadn't expected to like it, only trying the rice ball so as not to be rude, so I was surprised by how much I enjoyed it.

"That is good stuff. Thanks for sharing. I'd offer you some of my peanut butter sandwich but..." We both looked at the sad sandwich with distaste.

"No, thanks."

While I smirked and took another bite of my sandwich, I considered how to keep our conversation going. I had enjoyed being in class with her and envied how well she shot. She was knowledgeable and so fast on the draw. Half the time I'd hardly gotten my pistol out of the holster, and she was already three shots in.

"Nao, may I ask about your shooting experience? You're really kicking butt out there."

She had just taken a big bite of salad, and I recognized my timing was not ideal.

"Sorry, take your time."

She finished chewing and washed her bite down with some electrolyte water.

"I've been a competitive shooter for a couple of years. My ex-wife got me into it. She's a pro. Travels all over the country for shoots."

I froze mid-bite when I heard her say she had an ex-wife. I had not clocked her as a member of the rainbow family and was immediately rapt, saying the first thing that came to mind, and immediately knew it was lame. "Well, that's interesting."

Scrambling for a decent follow up, she rescued me by going on. "It's been fun. I switched over to a different event, so we don't usually run into each other. The divorce was not amicable, but you didn't ask."

I felt the need to reciprocate, since she had been open with me.

"I have one of those too. An ugly divorce, I mean. Not that I'm bragging, or anything." I scoffed, wishing I had kept my mouth shut. But since I had started, the avalanche of words tumbled out. "I shoot guns now as a way to let out all the pent-up energy I have from that. And to fill my free time."

She nodded knowingly and took another big bite of salad. I liked that she had a good appetite and was open to sharing personal things with me. A long dormant part of myself sat up and took notice. We finished our lunch, sitting side-by-side in companionable silence, watching the men smoke their vape pens and talk animatedly about hunting.

As the afternoon session started, they asked us to pick a partner. I immediately turned to Nao and raised my eyebrows. She gave me an assenting nod as I rose from my chair. The world spun briefly, and my hands tingled. Dehydration was settling in, despite the electrolyte water I had drunk during lunch. Nao gripped my upper arm firmly.

"Whoa, are you okay? You're swaying."

Her hand on my arm snapped me into full alert.

"I'm good. Just saw stars for a sec. I'll be fine."

"If you're sure. Let's go snag a good lane."

She jogged into the shooting bay and selected the lane on the end, which was beside a huge dividing wall made of lumber. The wall cast about six inches of shade, where I could stand when it wasn't my turn. I joined her, smiling.

The instructor told us to trade magazines, and we each hid three dummy rounds, called snap caps, in with the other person's ammunition. She was up first, and my job was simply to stand next to her and watch her hands. If she flinched when she pulled the trigger on a snap cap, I was supposed to make her do five dry fires before she could try again.

When they gave the 'all clear' to start firing, I stood off to her side, enjoying the fact I had a chance to truly look at her. Her features were small and sharply defined. Eyeing the target, she licked her lips, drew her pistol flawlessly and took aim, immediately taking a shot. She took her second shot without delay, which turned out to be a dummy round, but she didn't flinch.

She chuckled. "Nice try with the snap cap. But you didn't get me that time."

Thanks to my electronic earmuffs, I was easily able to hear her over everyone else's gunfire. She fired her third and fourth shots. The fourth was a snap cap, and her hands jerked up slightly.

"A flinch!" I announced victoriously.

She laughed and handed me her magazine, squeezing out five rock steady dry fires. I handed her back her magazine, and she finished it out without any issues.

We switched places, and I drew my pistol, knowing there were three snap caps hidden in it. She stood to my side, watching me closely.

The heat of the sun and being under her gaze drew sweat out of my pores. I squeezed off the first shot, which turned out to be a snap cap. Thankfully, I didn't waver and quickly ejected it. My second round was a bullet, which pierced the paper target millimeters from one of Nao's shots. I managed to make it through my entire magazine without having to pause for dry firing. Each of my shots landed immediately next to Nao's in a tight group.

One of the instructors, who had been standing behind me watching, stepped up to us.

"Would you look at that! You are both grouped so close together. Well done."

He clapped me on the back and moved on to the next pair. I stepped into the tiny bit of shade cast by the wall, hoping to get some relief from the sun radiating down on my back. My skin felt like it was somehow burning under my shirt.

Nao stood beside me. "You okay?"

"I'm good. I'll stick my face in front of the misting fan on our next break. Did you see our shots? I've never been able to group my rounds so tightly and definitely never been able to mirror someone else's shots like that."

She gave me a small grin. "We make a pretty great team, don't you think?"

"I do." I gave her the best smile I could muster even with my sun reddened cheeks and the oil slick of sunblock on my face. I realized it was hard to flirt when I was on my way to a sun stroke.

The other groups had to stop several times for dry fire practice, so it was a bit longer before the sound of gunfire stopped. We stood side by side watching them until the instructors called a cease fire and sent us for a water break. As we walked back to the shade tent, Nao looped her arm chummily through mine, sending my heart banging around my chest.

Reaching the misting fan, I stopped and chugged ice water in an effort to cool down. Nao approached, her cheeks rosy, and she wore a dripping wet bandana around her neck. I made space for her in front of the fan, motioning for her to join me. We stood hip-to-hip and cheek-to-cheek in front of the fan while it sprayed cool water on our faces.

I grimaced. "I hope I don't catch Legionnaires disease from breathing this mist in."

She let out a loud laugh. "You're something else, Dusty."

"Not the first time I've heard that. Hey, are you local?" I figured I needed to ask a few questions before I worked up the nerve to ask her on a date.

"I am. I live in town, just past those hills there." She pointed to the east.

"Do you have a long commute?" I knew I was digging, but she didn't have to answer if she didn't want.

Beads of water from the fan collected on the bill of my cap, dripping down the front of my shirt.

"Easy commute. I hop on the train and ride up a few stops, then walk a couple blocks to work. And because I know you want to ask, I'm a trauma nurse. Your turn."

"Me in a nutshell... I live just outside the old naval base in a cute little bungalow with my pup Rex and work as a mechanic for the fire department."

She nodded, and I swiped at the water drops collecting on my eyebrows. My body pulsed with the collective heat of the day, but at least my head was cool for a moment.

"A trauma nurse. That's the real deal. You must see... a lot."

"I do." She looked toward the large berm on the far side of the shooting bay and took a sip of water.

A distinct whistling sound passed by overhead. I flinched and looked up toward the top of the berm, following Nao's gaze. A puff of dust was dissipating in the breeze. Another whizzing whistle passed overhead, and a second puff of dust appeared atop the berm.

I took Nao by the arm and guided her until we stood behind a pillar.

"John?"

He looked up from the pocketknife he was fiddling with. "Yup."

"It sounds like someone is firing overhead. A pretty gnarly ricochet just winged past us."

He flapped a hand at me dismissively. "That's just the 200-yard range up top. They are shooting well above our heads. Nothing to worry about."

Our classmates went about their break unphased by the introduction of people shooting over our heads, so I did my best not to think too deeply about it. The last thing our range masters would want is someone getting shot, so I trusted John's dismissal of my concern.

Looking at Nao, I realized how close our bodies were, lined up behind the pillar. She gave me a smirk as her eyes traced my lips and throat. Desire zinged through me much like the ricocheting bullets overhead. I cleared my throat and took a step back, reminding myself that I was carrying a firearm and should not allow myself to get distracted.

"You ready to get back out there?"

"Sure."

We finished the afternoon session by running through timed drills and practicing our footwork. Normally a great shot when standing still, I found shooting while walking or side stepping to be challenging, and it was clear I needed practice. The whole group marveled at Nao's agility and speed as she navigated the course. I enjoyed watching her lithe body move effortlessly.

By the end she had outscored everyone and won a T-shirt for her efforts. The temperature at the range was to the point of nearly over-whelming me, so I was relieved when John released us.

I had no doubt I smelled terrible and looked even worse, but if I didn't say something I may never get another chance to see Nao. After locking up my pistols and securing my gear, I lingered until she started walking toward the parking lot. I jogged to catch up.

"Mind if I walk up with you?"

"Not at all. How did you like the class today?"

"It was fun. You?"

"Same. There's always something new to learn, and the practice is good."

We walked past one of the dynamic ranges where hot shots, dressed similarly to Nao, rapid fired at various targets while skirting obstacles.

I waited for a break in the gunfire and asked, "What do you think about us getting together sometime?"

"Honestly, Dusty, if you didn't ask me by the time we reached the parking lot I was going to ask you. So, good on you for getting up the nerve first."

I wiped at a drop of sweat the hung from my chin.

"Is that a *yes*?"

"It is."

Dimples creased her cheeks as we walked the last few yards to the parking lot. I paused, looking over all the vehicles, most of which were lifted pickup trucks with confederate flag tow hitches.

"Hang on. Let me guess." I spotted a Subaru with an RN sticker on the back window. "You're the Subaru, right?"

She chuckled. "And you're the Jeep, right?"

"I am. Good guess."

"It wasn't a guess at all. I was sitting in my car when you arrived this morning. You were in such a rush you didn't look around... and you looked kind of mean. I'm glad to know the first impression wasn't accurate."

My hot cheeks flushed more. She opened the rear hatch of her Subaru and placed her range bag inside. "So, us getting together. What do you have in mind?"

I shifted the weight of my bag as a bead of sweat slowly traveled down my side under my shirt.

"I'm open to just about anything, as long as we do it together."

She closed the rear hatch to her car and leaned against the bumper, which was probably the same temperature as the surface of the sun. "Together? Sounds good to me."

There was a pause as it seemed neither of us knew how to wrap things up. She surprised me by leaning in and giving me a hug. I hugged her back with my free arm. She smelled like gun oil and mint gum, which was an odor I could learn to love.

Two Bedrooms, One Bath, and a Ghost

Richard May

The house was a pale-yellow California bungalow just off La Cienega. The minute I walked inside I felt as if I'd already seen it. Maybe I had. I'd looked at a lot of houses. All my prospective new homes were beginning to merge in my brain.

"Perhaps in another life," the agent said gaily after I told her. She barked a halting, unconvincing laugh and continued to show me the space room-by-room, talking all the while about "potential," "original detail," and "period." She finished by opening the sliding glass door to the patio and ushering me outside. I gasped and stared with mouth wide open.

The backyard was a sensory riot, a medley of reds, yellows, oranges, purples, pinks, and greens. Visually overpowering. And the fragrance of so many flowers was deeply intoxicating. I wobbled slightly on my feet.

"Why don't we sit?" the agent suggested and, with a well-tanned hand tipped in glossy pink fingernails, indicated a small wrought-iron café table and two matching chairs. She settled herself onto one of them and opened her laptop. She was still perky and all smiles, but the cold eyes behind the designer glasses were ready for business. "The house is perfect, isn't it?" It wasn't a question.

I reviewed our passage through two sterile white bedrooms, one minuscule bath, a possible office, living room, dining room, and kitchen. I hadn't expected the Taj Mahal for the quoted price. I had some money to burn after selling the condo in New York but not enough for a forest fire. The house was within my budget, big enough, nice enough. *Enough* was the key word, but except for the garden, I was underwhelmed.

"You could always expand," she said, perhaps guessing size was the reason for my hesitancy. It probably had been for previous prospective buyers since she hadn't used the "we have several offers" ploy yet.

I looked at the beauty around us. "Oh, I wouldn't want to lose any of this."

She smiled, like a cat with a mouse in its paws. "This is lovely, isn't it?" she said, indicating the backyard with a broad sweep of her left arm and hand. She knew what might make the sale. "There are 53 roses. The work of decades."

"The house is small," I countered. Maybe she'd come down on the price. She'd have to if I was going to expand, as she put it.

"Just remember," my dad had told me as part of his advice on negotiation. "Go lower. It's been on the market for quite a while." Seven months, according to Redfin.

"You could build a second floor. Several new owners on the block have. It's a fantastic neighborhood." I mulled that feint over. A master bedroom upstairs with a balcony overlooking the roses. Maybe a circular staircase leading down to the patio. That was a thought, but did I have enough money? I wanted to be careful. New job, new debt. Old city though. I grew up in L.A. and had graduated from S.C. Then, it was off to New York.

I looked back at the house. A picture window framed a view of the dining room. I thought I saw someone move just out of view. Another prospective buyer? Didn't she have an exclusive? Probably a trick of the light.

I finished my survey of the backside of the cottage. The sliding glass door and another large window revealed most of the living room. *Good thing it's Los Angeles*, I said to myself. *The heating bills would be astronomical back in New York.*

The agent leaned toward me across her battleship-gray computer. She looked as if she had somewhere else to go. "Why don't you take a look around on your own. I'll be out here if you have any more questions."

I did as she prompted and wandered through again by myself. The feeling of familiarity returned, as if I'd lived here before or someone I knew had. A presence accompanied me throughout the redux. I felt an eagerness over my shoulder.

I wasn't much of a cook, so a small kitchen was no big deal. The dining room was just over a half wall. Linda was right: I could take that out. One big room *would* be much nicer. As she had mentioned, "So on trend." The "possible office" was highly doubtful. Closets were bigger, but New York had made me accustomed to living in less. There was room for a desk and a bookcase so why not give the closet a new title?

I considered the bathroom and reaffirmed my conclusion there was no room for renovation. Besides, I did like old tile and "classic" fixtures. But the bedrooms. They were... what? Maybe ten-by-twelve? *You could build higher*, a voice said in my head. It didn't sound like the agent's. Much deeper and less saccharine.

I returned to the living room and looked out the window. Linda was typing assiduously, using the time. Maybe she had given up on me and was booking another showing. I pivoted, taking in the twenty-by-twelve of the biggest room. I agreed with the voice; I could build up. Stairs would fit in the foyer. Small ones.

The screech of the sliding glass door startled the agent, but her smile quickly recovered. "Do you love it?" she asked, with a look that said of course I did.

"Why 53?" I asked as I approached the red table and chairs.

She blinked. "Oh. The roses. The previous owner planted one for every year he lived here."

"Wow! He lived here 53 years?"

"Yes," she answered slowly. She seemed unsure whether my response was positive or negative. She opted for positive. "One owner, so beautifully cared for." I loved that line, even though she had undoubtedly used it before. She gazed at the house. I thought of the garden. Both were immaculate, one in technicolor, the other monochromatic.

A warm breeze redolent of roses passed over me, like a caress. The fragrance helped me decide. "Linda, I want this place." I told her the price I was prepared to pay. She hesitated, thinking it over, then patted the empty chair beside her. I sat, and we wrote up an offer. Three days later, it was accepted. The heirs wanted to sell.

One advantage to moving from a condo into a small house was I didn't have to buy new furniture. My sister pointed that out to my father after I'd tried several times to convince him I hadn't made a mistake. "This place is way too small," he insisted. "You should have let me give it a looksee before you bought it."

"The garden is so big," my mother contributed, sounding just as negative.

"Jack won't have to buy anything new," Clare said in response to our father. "Besides, it's just him." I was glad she didn't add anything about it being five years since the last boyfriend. "And he can hire someone one to weed and whack," she assured my mother. That was my big sister, still always answering for me.

"So many roses," my mother mused. "It must get good sun."

"53," I said. "One for every year."

"Pardon me?"

I started to explain, but my father interrupted.

"You should build up," he prescribed in his CEO voice that dared anyone to disagree. I didn't tell him I'd already hired a contractor. "You have that extra money. Good thing the agent lowered the price."

"Because Jack made her," Clare said in more unasked-for defense.

While my family debated on my behalf without my participation, out of the corner of my eye, I saw him again. An elderly man, bending over to smell the Ebb Tide rose at the end of the central walkway. It was deep purple and full of the aroma of cinnamon and cloves. Frank, the previous owner. Who else could it be? "One owner, so beautifully cared for."

The old man looked up and smiled. I smiled back. I'd have to buy a new rose soon. His birthday was coming up. The agent had looked sideways at me when I asked his name and birthdate.

I realized my family was staring at me now.

"Shall we go in?" I suggested.

"When are the movers coming?" my father asked but turned toward the house without waiting for an answer. The three of them had driven over from Westwood and down from Santa Barbara to see the place and help me set up shop. Mom and Clare followed Dad up the steps to the small porch. I planned to widen it when I had the balcony built and staircase put in. I took another look at the garden. Frank was gone, but I wasn't worried. He'd be back. We were in this together now.

"The movers are here!" my father bellowed. I rushed up the narrow stairs in automatic response, but before I re-entered the house, I turned back toward the garden.

"See you later," I whispered.

THE DAY AFTER

VINCENT TRAUGHBER MEIS

Marcus bolted upright in bed and saw him standing in the room. He squeezed his eyes shut and fell back on the pillow. More than being afraid, he was leery. Before he let his emotions soar, he wanted to be sure it wasn't a dream. He slowly lifted his eyelids. He was still there. In his white hoodie. Hood up.

"You're not dreaming," said Zeke in that voice that was more than sound. Marcus felt it like a vibration passing through the air and taking hold of him. "I'm here."

With his pale face in shadow and his white clothes, it was still as if Marcus's imagination had conjured him. He needed to touch him.

"Come here," said Marcus, reaching out his hand.

Zeke took a step closer but was hesitant. "You know about me now."

"You didn't want me to? Is that why you ran away?"

"I didn't want you to be disappointed."

"But you're back."

"My mom told me I should."

Marcus smiled, remembering his conversation with her, the shocking revelation, and then her soothing voice in his ear, her hand on his head. "He visits me, too," she had said.

"Are you okay?" asked Marcus.

"Aside from, you know… I'm good… happy to see you again."

"Come. It's cold. Get under the covers." Marcus moved over and threw back the sheet and comforter."

"It won't help," he said dryly. "I'll still be cold. And I'll make you cold."

"We can pretend it's warm. Under the covers. It's just mind over matter."

Zeke sat on the edge of the bed and removed his sneakers that still looked new out of the box. He placed them neatly side-by-side just under the bed, leaned back, and slid into the opening Marcus had made for him. Marcus tucked him in and lay back, both of them staring at the ceiling, watching the shifting leaf patterns thanks to the streetlight coming through the branches of the tree outside his window, swayed by the wind off the ocean.

The early morning traffic had begun. A car slowed, followed by the soft thud of a newspaper on the stoop. The smell of someone's first cigarette of the day wafted up from the bus stop in front of the building. A truck screeched to a stop at the intersection, shifted gears, and moved on, rattling over a pothole. It was a normal day.

"How is your hand?" asked Zeke.

"It hurts. Do you want to kiss it to make it better?"

"I wish I could... make it better."

"Not one of your powers, huh?"

"I have no powers."

"That's debatable."

"I *see* a few things. Like about your parents. And just now, I passed by the ofrenda in the living room, the photos of your parents. Why did you deny it before?"

"You frightened me with your knowing things you couldn't have known."

"When I saw you dancing in the street and whirling like a dervish, it seemed you were trying to spin away all your pain."

The night before, Marcus and his friends had painted their faces and joined the Día de los Muertos procession through the Mission District. He had gotten caught up in the rhythm of a drumming group and started spinning. He soon found himself separated from his friends.

"My dad died a few months ago. My mom more than ten years ago. They both died young. Just so you know, longevity does not run in my family."

"Are you trying to scare me away?"

"It was a joke. A bad one. As if it would make a difference. Or maybe I will join you soon."

"Don't go there. Morbid humor makes me go cold."

"Sorry," Marcus said.

"Now, I'm joking."

He can joke. Good to know.

"One of my friends saw you. Identified you by your white hoodie."

"You must have a strong connection with him or her."

"Him, Sergio."

"Is he your boyfriend?"

"If I said yes, would you be jealous?"

Zeke turned to Marcus for the first time since he'd gotten into bed and smiled.

"That's a strange thing to say."

Marcus shifted onto his side, facing Zeke with his head resting on his palm. The faint pearly light of daybreak fell on Zeke's face. Marcus reached over and pushed the edge of the hood back so he could better see his dark curls tumbling down over his alabaster forehead, the pale lips he had kissed, the ice-blue eyes that lit up his soul.

"Would you consider popping back your hoodie?"

"You sound like my mom. 'Take that damn hood off,'" he said in a high-pitched imitation of his mother. He pushed the hood back and under his head.

"Much better. I can see you."

"So, is he?"

"Sergio?"

"Uh-huh."

"He would like to be, so everyone tells me."

"But you're waiting for something more, your *principe azul*."

"You know what's weird? In English we say your knight in shining armor. It's so militaristic. *Principe azul* sounds better. When I met your parents, I realized you were Latin, but you grew up here, right?"

"You checking my ethnic creds?"

"My mom was Mexican," said Marcus. "I didn't grow up speaking Spanish or anything, but I've made it my goal to learn. Making progress, I think."

"I was born here," said Zeke in a dreamy voice. "My parents are from Sonora, Mexico. We spoke Spanish at home."

Marcus touched Zeke's cheek. His skin was cool but soft. "You're so white."

"I was always light-skinned, you know... before... lighter than both of my parents and my sisters. Supposedly, we descended from Spanish aristocracy or some bullshit."

"Doesn't matter." Marcus ran his fingers across Zeke's forehead and down his nose to his lips. They looked bluish in the pale light. "Can I kiss you?"

"Are you sure? I mean... maybe we should talk more."

"Like favorite color? Favorite song? I thought we were beyond that shit."

"We are. I just mean... come on. It's got to be weird for you."

"Is getting to know someone ever not weird?"

Zeke drifted into stillness. He looked to be staring at the ceiling, but Marcus wasn't sure. He could have been staring into that place he could go and Marcus couldn't, suspended between here and there. Marcus didn't know how to react. He didn't want to mess with this wrinkle in time or whatever it was. He lay back and tried to make himself comfortable as if they were meditating side-by-side.

After several minutes of lying completely still, Marcus became impatient. "Ezekiel," he said softly but firmly, pronouncing it in Spanish.

Zeke appeared startled, but it was successful in bringing him back. "You sounded like my father. Only my parents call me that."

"I wasn't even sure that was your name. I guessed."

"On some level you knew... knew it would reach me."

"Sort of a safe word in reverse, not to get out of something, but to get back in."

"Ah," said Zeke, shaking his shoulders back and forth, showing his joy. "I like you so much. I felt it the moment I saw you."

"Sometimes I think you're messing with me."

"I told you I'd never do that. What would be the point?"

Marcus leaned over, and when their lips came together, it was shocking to him at first, the coolness, even though he had already experienced it in that first kiss the night before. But when Zeke put a hand very gently on the back of his head and pulled him close, it didn't matter. Mind over matter. His heart was working hard as if pumping for both of them. He imagined Zeke absorbing his warmth, and like the fairy with the turquoise hair making Pinocchio a real boy, he would breathe life into him.

Zeke broke the kiss and pulled Marcus's head to his chest. "Sorry."

"For what?"

"It must be strange for you. Now that you know."

"Not really thinking about it. When it feels good with someone, you just flow with it."

"You have a lot of experience just flowing with it?"

"Very little actually. What about you?"

"Same. Like I told you last night, I was drawn to you. I didn't have a plan. In that short time we were together, it was like we had always been together. Then your friends showed up, and I thought you didn't need me, that what I was doing wasn't good, that I could hurt you."

A theory brewed in Marcus's head. Zeke needed him to be connected to what he had lost. And he was happy to be the conduit. It gave him a purpose that he seemed lacking in life. And though he was content to stay in bed all day, holding Zeke, exchanging thoughts, sometimes in words and sometimes in direct transfer, he wondered if he was being selfish.

"Is there anything you want to do today?" asked Marcus. "Anyplace you want to go?"

"Do you know the gourmet donut shop on 24th Street?"

Marcus patted his stomach. "Where do you think this came from? I'm always up for a maple glazed bacon apple."

"I knew you were a bad boy," he said with a laugh that was pure joy. Infectious.

"You laughed!"

"I can laugh. I used to laugh a lot."

"God, I wish I had known you..."

Zeke put his cool fingers over Marcus's mouth. "We met when we did. *Finito.*"

Marcus's phone pinged with a message. He reached over Zeke to the bedside table. "Sorry. It might be my boss."

"That's right. You're a working man."

"I was supposed to work from home today." He opened his phone and read the text. Sighed.

"What?"

"It's Sergio. He insists on taking me to the clinic where he works to have someone look at my hand. He's on his way over here."

"The donuts will have to wait. I'll discreetly sneak out the back door."

"There is no back door."

Zeke laughed. The second time in a few minutes. "Meet you at the donut shop at three. Text me if you're going to be late." That cool, sparkling laugh again. Third of the day.

His doorbell rang and he walked down the long hall. Before he opened the door, he looked back toward his bedroom even though he knew Zeke was already gone. He exhaled. Three in the afternoon wasn't that far away.

Sergio held two cups of coffee in a holder and a grease-stained brown paper bag Marcus recognized as being from the donut shop.

"I got you that maple thingy you like."

"Serge, that was so sweet," Marcus said in a syrupy but genuine voice. "Come in. Sit."

His friends had done a good job of cleaning up. All the face paint, brushes and makeup utensils were in a shoebox on a corner of the table. But they had missed a few sequins and some glitter on the chair he pulled out for Sergio. "Wait." He brushed the sparkly things onto the floor and giggled. "Don't want you to have glitter ass."

Sergio looked at him suspiciously as if not used to Marcus being so nice to him. "You sound buzzed. In a happy kind of way. Last night you were kinda trippin'. We were worried."

"All good."

"Let me see your hand." They sat at the kitchen table and Sergio examined his bandaged hand.

"See. I didn't bleed out."

"*Culero*, don't even say that. Still think we should have someone look at it."

Marcus grabbed his coffee and took a sip. "Sure. Let's go. I've got things to do. I'm a working man," he said with the thrill of echoing Zeke's words.

Sergio again looked at him from under a wrinkled forehead and thick eyebrows as if surprised at Marcus's lack of protest. The night before he had absolutely refused to attend to the cut he had sustained when he tripped, carrying a glass vase of flowers to the Day of the Dead altar for his parents.

"Don't you want your donut?" said Sergio.

Marcus took the caramel-colored, bacon-bit-encrusted donut out of the bag and frowned. He was supposed to be having this experience with Zeke.

"You gone veggie or something? You're looking at it like it's going to kill you."

"No way. The veggie part. Kill me, it might." He took a big bite to show his appreciation for Sergio going to all the trouble. As Sergio looked on with almost erotic interest, his eyes wide and his mouth hanging open, the flavors exploded in Marcus's mouth, sweet, salty, crispy fat, and the comfort of maple. He offered Sergio a bite.

He shook his head. "Thanks. Already ate. You enjoy it."

A short time later, they were walking along Folsom Street to the clinic. They spotted mangled Day of the Dead decorations, mostly burned candles on a stoop, and a few trampled marigolds in the gutter. They saw a group of women dressed in black, wearing lace veils and holding bouquets of flowers, probably on their way to the cemetery.

"What was going on with you last night?" asked Sergio.

"I guess thinking about my dad made me out of whack. You know, first Día de los Muertos without him."

"Yeah, of course. But, I mean, that guy you met. And then that couple you talked to. Was there some connection?"

Marcus shook his coffee cup and then swallowed the last of it. "No. I just felt sad for them losing their son."

"You said something about kissing the guy in the photo."

After his encounter with Zeke in the alley, Marcus and his friends had gone to the park where the Day of the Dead ofrendas were set up, tables large and small with lots of candles, photos of various family members, and covered with bouquets of flowers, trinkets, and favorite foods of the deceased. They had wandered the park along with the other marchers from the procession. Drummers had assembled in one corner of the square, joined by others with cowbells, tambourines, maracas, and gongs. Smoke spiraled into the air from fire pits, candles, and people smoking cigarettes and joints. It was tribal and rhythmic with most people's true identities hidden by masks and makeup. The atmosphere was otherworldly.

Marcus had spotted a woman who sat behind a small altar with her husband. He was drawn to her enigmatic smile, which had a certain familiarity. He approached the small table with a single framed picture illuminated by a candle and recognized Zeke in the photo. He would have collapsed if Sergio, Ash, and Jane hadn't caught him.

"Serge, why are you making such a big deal out of this? It was a weird night. It's over."

"Fer and Jane have a theory."

"Of course they do. Wait, they agree on something."

"Bizarre, huh? They think..."

"Stop. I don't want to hear it."

"...you made it up to..."

"I'm serious. I could care less what they think. I talked to some guy. He disappeared. I had a sad moment with that couple. End of story. Can we just fucking drop it?"

Sergio's eyes popped as if slapped by Marcus's harsh tone. "All right! Sorry." They had arrived in front of the clinic where Sergio worked as a nurse. "Come on. Let's have someone look at your hand and see if you need stitches."

Marcus lay a hand on Sergio's arm. "I'm *conmovido* by your concern, *de verdad*. Y'all take care of me."

"Of course. We love you, man."

Marcus knew he was lucky to have amigos like Sergio, Jane, Fer, Josh, Ash, and Pats, especially Sergio who would do anything for him. They had taken him home after his freakout, put him to bed, and cleaned up the mess in his apartment from the face painting. He felt bad he couldn't share with them what had happened when the Batalá drummers of the procession had made him go into one of his absences and he got separated from them, how he had ducked into an alley for a breather, how Zeke had come into his life, and how he had reappeared that morning. How could they understand that he needed Zeke and Zeke needed him?

They walked through the clinic waiting room and several heads lifted up, people no doubt who had been waiting since the clinic opened. Marcus felt guilty that he was walked right in.

With new stitches in his hand, Marcus walked home, hoping he wouldn't be too distracted by his three o'clock date to work.

With his tech skills, he had gotten a job at Airbnb. Recently, there had been complaints about the Airbnb hosting app, and as the project manager for the app, it was his responsibility to fix it. His work seemed so unimportant in the greater scheme of things, especially now. He felt he was embarking on a new phase in his life.

Marcus was giddy when he saw Zeke, hood up, sitting on the bench in front of the donut shop. "What should we get?" asked Marcus.

"I'm trying to cut down on sugar," Zeke said with a chuckle. "You go ahead,"

"Yeah. Right. I wasn't trying to be funny. I was just so excited to see you and nervous and thankful and..."

"I get it, *cariño*."

Marcus's jaw fell and his heart bounced. *Cariño*, he had called him.

"Go on," said Zeke. "Ask for Andres. Tell him you're a friend of mine."

"Is Andres here?" Marcus said to the young woman with turquoise hair and a nose ring on the other side of the window.

"Andy," she shouted through a tiny window behind her. "Somebody here to see you."

A man came from the back who could have been Zeke's brother though a little heftier and with skin a tiny shade less white. "Can I help you?"

"I'm a friend of Zeke's."

Andres took a step back and turned paler still. He looked over and around Marcus as if expecting to see Zeke behind him. He squinted and his shoulders tensed. "So, what do you want?" he growled in such a gruff manner it caused the woman to gawk in surprise.

"A... a donut?"

"Rosie will help you. I'm kinda busy." He made an angry about-face and returned to the back.

Rosie shrugged. "What can I get ya?"

Marcus had lost his appetite but felt obliged to order something. Andres's reaction was over the top. Something weird was happening. "What's that one?" He pointed at a cake donut in the wood and glass display case with white icing and embedded with red and green bits.

"That's a jalapeño lime. It's kickass."

"One of those," he said mechanically. While she wrapped it up, he turned around and looked at Zeke on the bench who was staring at the ground between his feet.

He paid and walked back over to Zeke. "What was that all about?"

"Sorry. I shouldn't have done that, put you in that position."

"Why was he so pissed off?"

"It's com–"

"Don't say complicated. I hate it when people do that."

Zeke motioned for him to sit on the bench. "He's my brother from another mother. I helped him get this business going. We worked our asses off and look at the place now."

"Were you like lovers?"

"No. I loved him like *mi hermano*. I tried to visit him once. He wigged out. He yelled at me and cursed me and cried like a baby. I left. Couldn't stand seeing him in so much pain. I thought maybe if you became friends with him, you could tell him I'm okay and I love him forever. Stupid idea, I guess."

"The idea's not stupid. But you could have warned me."

"We were supposed to do that swim for my birthday together, but we had an argument the day before. I think he blames himself."

Zeke looked like he might cry. Could he cry?

"Let's go back to my place."

They trudged along the nearly empty streets to Marcus's apartment. The afternoon had turned foggy, and the wind blew a chill through Marcus.

When they got inside, Marcus dropped the uneaten donut on the table and turned the thermostat up, bringing the wall furnace to life. He felt a chill in his bones that only getting under the bed covers or a hot bath could alleviate. With Zeke, getting under the covers seemed the better option. Marcus took Zeke's hand and led him to the bed. Marcus hugged him. "Don't worry about Andres. He'll be okay."

"I want to do something," Zeke said or projected into Marcus's mind, that vibration thing he did that was as much a feeling as words. Marcus felt it in every fiber of his body. It needed no explanation. He reached for the hem of Zeke's sweatshirt and slowly began to lift it, his hands shaking, unsure what he would find under the clothes. So far, he had only seen Zeke's face and hands. But it was always the case, he reasoned, the doubt and excitement and curiosity the first time you laid eyes on someone's body. But the stakes were higher here, the agency he would have more overpowering.

"Yes, this," said Zeke, as he lifted his arms up, letting Marcus pull the hoodie over his head. The T-shirt he wore under it was a dazzling white in the gray, foggy afternoon.

"One layer down," Marcus said, looking into Zeke's clear blue eyes, watching for a sign for him to stop. Zeke was now more present than he had ever been, open, his lips slightly parted.

"Keep going," he whispered.

Marcus removed the T-shirt, revealing skin whiter than the shirt, hairless, flat stomach, a swimmer's body. He dropped the shirt on the floor and ran his hands over Zeke's torso from his chin down to his waist.

Zeke winced. "I'm hella ticklish," he said with a smile.

Marcus removed his own sweater and T-shirt in one swift motion. He pulled Zeke into a hug, pressing their chests together, the coolness of Zeke's body no longer an issue as nature took its course, making him hard. "Does everything... like... work?"

Zeke's shoulders lifted in a half-shrug. "I guess we'll find out."

They finished undressing and Marcus took a step back to examine the statue in front of him. Zeke's physique and hand on his waist were reminiscent of Donatello's David, but the classical nose, mop of curly hair, and distant look were all Michelangelo's. "Let's get into bed," said Marcus. "That heater isn't doing shit."

They spent a lot of time kissing, touching. They licked each other like dogs. And yes, everything worked. Marcus understood without any exchange of words that Zeke wanted Marcus inside him. Everything progressed naturally from understanding to the joining of bodies. It was like sex in a dream, all sensation and nothing messy. No condom negotiation, no fear of disease. Looking down at Zeke's face as he entered him, Marcus experienced an ecstasy on a higher plane, a constant rush up and down his body, again like a dream where he was flying through the air. Gone was the desire-driven pumping and grinding to reach the end goal of orgasm. This was using each other's bodies to be suspended outside them, not unlike his absences or as the doctors called them, his *petit mals*.

After a time, impossible to know how long, Marcus needed to stretch his muscles, and he fell to Zeke's side. He pulled Zeke's head to his chest, the black curls brushing his skin, prompting yet more explosive sensations.

"You are my first and only," Zeke whispered.

"You mean...?"

"Another thing I never got to do."

The sweetness of it brought Marcus to tears, his eyes filling, overwhelmed by emotions he had never experienced. In a shaky voice, he said, "Not my first, but the only one that mattered."

The room was completely dark when Marcus awoke. He was alone. The apartment was now stifling. He threw off the covers. "Zeke?" He didn't expect an answer.

Marcus approached the donut shop window. "Hi, Rosie. Is Andres here?"

She shook her head.

"Not here, or doesn't want to talk to me?"

She nodded toward the back.

He walked inside the store where there were a few tables and into the kitchen.

Andres turned around quickly. "This is a restricted... oh, it's you."

"It's not your fault, you know."

"What the fuck are you talking about?"

"Zeke doesn't blame you."

"Get the fuck out!"

"He wants you to know he's okay and loves you and wants you to be okay."

Andres was momentarily stunned. He put his hands under the upper part of his apron as if to protect his heart. He stared at Marcus a long time. "You're full of shit."

"I may be, but not about this."

"You're a friend of his? He never mentioned you."

"I've only known him a few days."

Andres removed his hands from under his apron, clenched his fists, and took a step toward Marcus. "Now I know you're out of your freaking mind. He's dead, man. Has been for months."

"He visits me."

Andres squeezed his eyes shut. "Please. Just leave."

"He told me about your trip to Europe. The night on the beach in Santorini."

Andres's gray eyes popped open and searched the surroundings as if he might find some logical explanation. The exhaust fan rattled. A motorcycle screamed by outside. "We swore never to tell anybody," he said in a near whisper. "He told you?"

"But it wasn't like he really told me, was it? It means everything to him that you two are good."

"No, no, no, no, no. This is not happening." Agony was painted on his face, but Marcus could see the wall was cracking. The first hint of belief was emerging.

"You don't think it's strange for me?" said Marcus. "Things have happened that make no fucking sense. I'm not crazy, but I must have a vulnerability that he was able to use, in part to get to you."

Andres slumped onto a stool at the worktable and put his head in his hands. He began to weep quietly. "He was more than a best friend, but to say he was my brother doesn't really capture it either," he said in a voice full of mucus. "And yet we couldn't be lovers despite loving each other more than anyone on this earth. We realized it that night on the beach in Greece. He would only have told you about that night if he had to."

"I now wonder if he's interested in me at all, or he's just using me to get to you."

Andres raised his head with a half-smile and wiped his eyes. "You're totally his type. He rarely met anyone he liked. Me neither. That's why we thought, at least for one night, that maybe we should be together. But... no."

Marcus moved close to him and put a hand on his shoulder. At first, he flinched, but then accepted it, leaned into it as if it would bring him closer to Zeke. He believed. "So, you talk to him and stuff?"

"And stuff."

"Don't tell me you've slept together."

"Uh..."

"No fucking way. He wanted that kind of love so bad." Andres took hold of Marcus's hand still on his shoulder. "Sorry I yelled at you before."

"Understandable."

"Tell him I'm sorry I freaked out when he came to me. Tell him I'll love him until the day I die. And tell him he's a fucking *pendejo* for checking out and not giving me a chance to say goodbye."

"I will. I gotta go," Marcus said, pursing his lips. "He might... uh... be coming over."

"Stop by anytime. Tell me *que pasa*, ya know. Donuts on the house."

Marcus and Zeke sat on the hill at the southwest corner of Dolores Park. They had been spending most nights together except for a couple of times Zeke went to visit his parents. They had gone to a lot of Zeke's favorite places, many of which turned out to be Marcus's favorite places.

It was a warm day, and below them were people in various stages of undress, soaking up the sun, dotting the landscape like shiny hard rock candies. Beyond them was one of the most dope views of the San Francisco skyline with the Mission High Spanish Baroque tower in the foreground.

"I love this view," said Marcus. "I used to cut class just so I could come up here and daydream."

"I went to school there, too. I was a few years behind you."

"I met some of my best friends there, Sergio, Josh, Fer. We were a band of misfits that hung together for survival. It's funny all the guys in my friend group are from high school. Most of my women friends I met at San Francisco State. I brought them all together into a hive. There was some... hmm... cross pollination, but mostly we're just friends."

"It's nice to have friends," Zeke said dreamily.

"I went to see Andres."

"I know."

"I think he got it after he calmed down and stopped yelling at me to get out. He had a moment. Said he'd love you until the day he died."

"Not after?" Zeke said with a chuckle, but he seemed pleased enough that he pushed his hood back and let his curls tumble out, which he almost never did outside the apartment. "What do you think of him?"

"Andres? What do you mean?"

"Do you like him?"

"He's cool. I left him in a good state."

Zeke nodded and smiled. "You're not gonna find a better man on this earth."

Marcus wasn't sure where this was going. He couldn't think about anyone but Zeke. "I know. Any man that offers me free donuts is *mi hermano para siempre*," he said, smoothing his panic with a little humor.

"You guys should hang out."

"Yeah, sure," said Marcus, rising quickly to his feet. "I have to get back. I'm supposed to be on a work Zoom at 4:00."

"I'll walk you home, but I won't come in."

"Why not?"

"Because." Marcus had learned not to push him if he wasn't upfront with an answer.

They walked in silence over the hill to 24th Street and then down into the heart of the Mission, crossing through Balmy Alley where they had met. Marcus stopped to look at the mural of the indigenous women holding their fists in the air, the exact place Zeke first spoke to him. He had sat on the ground to rest from the chaos in the streets and in his head when Zeke approached him out of the blue to ask if he was okay.

Marcus turned around to comment on the woman who held a child in one arm while the other was raised in protest. But Zeke was gone. Marcus had gotten used to Zeke's sudden comings and goings. He had no choice. Something he couldn't control and wasn't sure if Zeke could either.

He reached his apartment and put the key in the lock. As soon as he pushed the door open, he heard people talking. He recognized Jane's gravelly voice. In the living room was his group, *la colmena*, they called themselves, his family of friends.

"What the hell?"

"Sorry for the sneak attack," said Pats. "Jane had a key."

Marcus looked around the room. "Where's Sergio?" He was the only one missing.

"He didn't want to participate," said Ash.

"Participate in what?"

"*Hermano*," said Fer, "you been off the radar, and we been sweatin' your lack of communication."

"Nobody's heard from you since los muertos," said Jane. "You haven't answered any of our texts."

"You guys know I do the walkabout from time to time. No biggie."

"This is weird, even for you," said Josh. "That night you went all paranormal on us, freaking out those poor people at the park."

"Is it your dad?" said Pats. "We all miss Henry tons. Not like you, I'm sure, but..."

Marcus fell into the empty chair someone had brought in from the kitchen table for what seemed an interrogation. He threw his head back and stared at the ceiling. "It's been hard, but I'm fine now."

"Have you been eating?" said Ash. "Your fridge is like vacay mode. We picked up some tacos."

"Guys, please. Nothing is going on. I'm fine."

"You met someone that night and been shacking up," said Fer. "That's what I think."

Marcus tried not to react. "Did Serge tell you that?"

"He loves you, man," said Josh.

"I love him too. But here's the skinny on that, which you already know. Not gonna happen. So, please, stop pushing it."

Marcus managed to convince them everything was cool and they ate tacos and drank beers and he completely spaced on his work Zoom. At around 9:00, Marcus started hinting he was tired, but Fer got the idea to go to the corner store and buy a bottle of tequila.

Marcus's façade that everything was peachy was beginning to crack. Plus, he couldn't stop thinking about his conversation with Zeke earlier. What was all that nonsense about liking Andres, and saying they should hang out like he was trying to get them to hook up? The more he thought about it the weirder he felt. He knew Zeke couldn't visit as long as the gang was there, so he had to get rid of them without them going all woo-woo he was going to slit his wrists as soon as they left. He needed to clarify things with Zeke.

It was 11:30 by the time he convinced them to leave, saying he had to work in the morning. He assured them with hugs and I-love-yous that everything was cool, and they needn't worry. Fer was so drunk he had passed out on the sofa, and Marcus panicked that he was going to stay until Josh pulled him to his feet. They both gave him sloppy kisses on the mouth at the door. Pats began talking about how much she missed Henry and then started crying as she often did when she got drunk.

When Marcus came out of the bathroom after brushing his teeth, Zeke was sitting on the side of the bed. "God, I'm so glad to see you. I thought I'd never get rid of them." He took Zeke's hand and pulled him up into a hug. He reached up from behind and pulled the hood off Zeke's head. Zeke put it back on. "What's wrong?" said Marcus.

"I have to go," Zeke said quietly.

"To your parents? Can we talk first?"

"Not to my parents. I mean, for good."

Marcus's whole body began to shake. "You don't mean that. This is good. I love every minute of being with you. I love you!" It was the first time he had uttered those words in that way. The thought of losing him made the tears begin to flow.

"Don't, *cariño*. I love you too. But it can't go on. You must see that."

"You're breaking up with me?" he wailed. "Don't I get a say in this?"

Zeke shot him a look, not unkind, but forceful, certain.

"I don't care if people think I'm going insane. You are everything to me."

Zeke shook his head. "I can't be everything to you. You know that."

Zeke held him as he sobbed his way to acceptance. He kissed Marcus's tears. "You must do one thing for me. Go to Andres. Tell him goodbye for me."

"Tell him yourself!" Marcus said as if a last-ditch anger might change the course of what was happening.

"Do this for me."

On the cusp of day but still dark, Marcus was at the metal security door at the back of the donut shop. The intoxicating aroma of fresh donuts filled the air. The exhaust fan rattled. A figure moved about the kitchen, happily in his element, sure of his movements. He lifted his head and saw Marcus. "I thought you were a homeless person at first."

"*Mas o menos.*"

Andres unlocked the door and waved Marcus in. "Oh, come now. Is it all that bad?"

"He broke up with me."

Andres grinned. "Do you have any idea how that sounds?"

"Fucking insane."

"There's a fix for that. Come in and sit. I'll get you a coffee."

"You're laughing at me, but you're the one who looks ridiculous with like a fucking constellation of flour across your cheek." Marcus brushed his hand over his own cheek to show where it was.

Andres turned his face toward Marcus as if expecting him to brush it off. "Help me out then, amigo."

Marcus lightly swept his fingers over Andres's cheek. "There." He slumped onto a stool.

"I get it," said Andres. "Everyone was in love with Zeke. Just realize it was you he chose."

"More like use."

"I know you don't feel that way, *de verdad.* You had this time, this moment of love. There's beauty in that."

"You're as insane as I am to believe that this even happened."

"That first time you came to me with this loco story about being his friend, it made me angry, yeah. Mostly because I saw something in your eyes like a reflection of him and I knew it was true. I had a hard time with it. I'm not laughing at you but at the limited capacity we have to believe shit that doesn't fit into what we've been taught. He did this for a reason."

"It fucked me up, man."

"No, it didn't. It gave you a new direction. I can see how it affected you." Andres poured a cup of coffee and put it in front of him. "Milk? Sugar?"

"Black is good."

Andres pulled up another stool and they sat in silence, sipping their coffee.

"Would you like to go out for a drink tomorrow night?" said Andres. "The shop is closed on Sunday."

"I don't know. I'm not much of a drinker."

"Bobo, I'm asking you out."

"Oh. Because that's what he would have wanted?"

"No. I'm asking because it's what I want. I want to go out with you. *Tu y yo.* Just us."

Marcus twisted his mouth in confusion, staring at the worktable, resisting for no reason.

"Oye, don't leave me hanging," said Andres.

Marcus turned to him with a smile. "Bueno. Why not? You and me." He nodded his head slowly. "Yeah." He glanced at the rack of donuts.

"You want one of those?" Andres said, pointing at a tray of maple glazed bacon apple.

"It seems too early."

"It's not." He got up, grabbed a donut, and put it in front of Marcus. "We created this one together."

"You and Zeke?"

"Yeah. And now you get to enjoy it." With a sweet smile, he reached up and moved the hair off Marcus's forehead, letting his fingers slide down his cheek.

As they gazed at each other with curiosity, the shelf above the work-table began to shake like in a small earthquake. A bowl tumbled down, scattering a galaxy of multi-colored sprinkles across the table. After the initial shock, Marcus and Andres stared at the colorful display and broke into laughter. They weren't alone.

ADRIFT

M.D. NEU

We often think of being together with our friends and loved ones as the ultimate goal,
but what if that isn't the case?
What if being together with the one we love most is no longer a dream, but a
nightmare?

The sun continued to lower in the west, casting a golden hue over the
endless expanse of the Pacific Ocean. For his entire life, this was the only
view Alex ever wanted. What was the old saying? *Give me a strong ship and
a star to sail her by.* Buying the *Seaduction*, even second hand, was a fulfill-
ment of that dream. But now, now that he lived this life, he wanted to be
on dry land again. He wanted to be around other people. He wanted to be
back in San Jose, rushing around Santana Row, seeing a baseball game at
the San Jose Giants stadium, riding his bike in Alum Rock Park, or on the
Los Gatos Creek Trail. All the things he thought he wanted to get away
from, he now missed.

Alex adjusted his glasses as he continued to pull down the sails and
secure them for the night. With a sigh, he looked out at the big blue. The
gentle lapping of the waves against the hull of the sailboat were now the
only sound breaking the serene silence, a relentless reminder of what he
missed.

"Spending all my time on racing boats off the coast, learning everything I could... and now..." Alex huffed the words out to remind himself
that he still had a voice. He secured the last line before checking the
anchor and ensuring the dinghy's cabin was secure.

As if thunder clapped and swells beat against the side of the boat,
Jacob began to emerge from below deck singing.

"Who else am I gon' lean on when times get rough?
Who's going to talk to me on
The phone 'til the sun comes up?"

"Don't you know any other songs?" Alex snapped, standing to his full
height and waiting for Jacob to reveal himself.

"I thought you liked Mariah Carey?" Jacob fully emerged from below
deck. He was naked as usual, the only material acting like a cover was a
blue towel hanging around his neck. His body was not what it once had
been, but whose was? Age and not being able to go to the gym four times
a week would do that to a person. Jacob hadn't really let himself go, but
since he wasn't handy on the sailboat, no matter what Alex tried, he didn't
get as much physical activity as Alex.

But sailing was never Jacob's thing, it was mine. Still, he could at least try.

"You know you're gonna get a sunburn... again." Alex waved a hand in Jacob's direction. Even in his annoyance, he wouldn't complain about the view, no matter what, he did appreciate seeing Jacob au naturel.

"I'm fine. Plus, I've got you to rub lotion on me."

The comment to anyone else would have been a flirtation, but with the tilt of Jacob's brow and the lack of smile on his lips, it was anything but seductive.

"I'm busy..." Alex moved around the deck, ensuring everything was secure for the night.

"You're always busy. If you're not steering the ship..."

"Boat."

"Whatever." Jacob huffed and pulled the towel from his neck, then placed it between the plastic tubs holding their vegetable garden and the other two tubs that they used to filter the sea water into drinking water. "This ship..."

"Boat."

"Yacht... has become your whole life."

"Because this *sailboat* is the only thing keeping us safe and alive."

"It's been over a year." Jacob laid down on the towel, adjusting so he could watch the ocean and the sky.

"And we're still alive, and I'd like to keep us that way." Alex surveyed the ocean, but there was nothing. He pulled off his glasses, rubbed his eyes, and then replaced his glasses on his face before scanning the area again.

"And I'm grateful for everything you do for us, but..."

Alex bit back the snark that wanted to rush from his lips. He took a breath and glanced out at the water again. "Did you hear anything on the radio today?" he asked before Jacob was able to finish his response.

"No. I thought maybe, but it was the same old repeated message from the Navy... I was hoping since we're getting close to the San Francisco Bay, we could go in there again and see if there's anything."

"The last time we were there, we almost died."

"But we ended up with the solar panels and the seeds so we could have our little garden." Jacob pointed to the makeshift vegetable garden they had.

The peppers, tomatoes, radishes, carrots, lettuce, broccoli, strawberries, and herbs weren't plentiful, but they helped them get by, along with the fishing they were able to do.

It's amazing how quickly you learn to love foods you once hated if it meant you wouldn't starve.

"If we went back ashore, we might be able to find a few more bins we can use as planters." Jacob continued. "And I still think building some kind of raft next to the boat might give us more room for –"

"We wouldn't be able to keep a raft connected if there was a storm. You remember the last nasty storm? We almost sunk."

"But we didn't, thanks to you." Jacob beamed at Alex.

The first honest expression of gratitude I've seen in a while.

Alex's stomach dropped. What happened to them? They were so close. He once loved being on the *Seaduction* alone with Jacob. Now... "It wasn't only me, you helped." he said, not allowing anymore negative thoughts to fill his mind.

Jacob barked out a laugh. "I held on to the wheel crying, praying we didn't sink."

"Well, with you on the wheel, I was able to handle the rigging and ensure we didn't lose our sail... again."

"That wasn't my fault." Jacob pointed at Alex with two fingers.

"I didn't say it was."

"But you –"

"Please, I don't want to fight."

Jacob crossed his arms over his chest. "Don't you? That seems like the only thing you ever want to do anymore. You know we're in this together."

"That's not fair."

"*Fair*? None of this is fair! You think I want to be trapped on this sail-boat? I miss going out. I miss our friends. I even miss my job. Hell, I miss how we used to have sex. There isn't a place on this boat that we didn't go at it, and now..."

"The world's changed." Alex fussed with his glasses.

"No shit..." Jacob laughed as he pushed some of his blond hair from over his eyes. "If it wasn't for me, we'd probably be dead. I was the one that called you that day. I was the one that told you something was happening and you –"

"And I didn't believe you." Alex rubbed his clean-shaven chin. Jacob wasn't wrong. He worked for the county and they got a heads up, of sorts, as to what was going on, but everyone thought and believed the government. They assumed the military could handle it. Clearly, everyone was wrong.

Including me.

Jacob didn't speak anymore, deciding instead to hum and lay out enjoying the ever-lessening sunlight. Alex glanced over, seeing Jacob's naked form glistening in the late afternoon sunlight. The golden hues enhanced his bronzed skin and highlighted the bleach blond hair atop his head. Alex closed his eyes, remembering how it once had been between them, and how much he wanted to experience that again.

He looked out to sea; there was nothing. There never was. Well, not in months. Off in the distance, to the East, he saw a few outcroppings of land. They didn't need to go out too far, just far enough to not be seen, and he liked being able to flee if they needed to.

Despite my feelings, this sailboat is fast, and we can get out of places in a hurry if need be.

Today the ocean had been calm, enough breeze to keep them moving, luckily the water didn't have the chop it could have. Glancing around, Alex saw everything was secure for the coming night. He snuck another peek at Jacob, who proudly lay naked as the day he was born. He had always been so comfortable in his skin, something Alex never was. He decided he needed to make an effort, even if it was to only fulfill their current physical needs. Luckily when Jacob was in a mood, he had a way of tuning everything and everyone out. So, by the time Alex was fully undressed, standing over Jacob and casting him in a shadow, that was the only thing that got Jacob's attention.

"Do you mind?" Jacob scowled before opening his eyes.

"If you want, I can go back to what I was doing, but I thought you might want to..."

Jacob's eyes opened wider, and a smile blossomed across his lips. Alex stood naked and semi-aroused, only wearing his glasses.

"I want you to know that I heard you and... well... I'm sorry." He fretted with his glasses.

"So, you're sorry? Well, you certainly know how to apologize... now come here and kiss me." Jacob reached out a hand to Alex and pulled him toward him.

Despite all the fussing and fighting, the one thing Alex and Jacob always understood about the other was how to satisfy each other. Their lovemaking under the golden light of dusk lasted until the bitter dampness of the night closed in around them like a frosty blanket.

No fog tonight, or at least so far.

Alex stretched out, replacing his glasses as Jacob cuddled next to him. He wished they could stay in this moment forever, just the two of them, like it was in the olden days.

Below deck, they were both dressed and sitting at the galley table eating their cooked halibut accompanied by carrot and radish salad. It wasn't exciting or like anything you'd find at a five-star restaurant, but the meal was good and the longer they spent out at sea, the better chefs they became with what the ocean supplied them.

"I have a surprise." Jacob got up from the table and rushed to the galley refrigerator, then pulled out two small bowls of strawberries. "There aren't a ton, but..." He shrugged, placing the small bowl down in front of Alex.

"These look amazing."

"We'll have more in a few days." Jacob sat back down. "So, I figured tonight we can treat ourselves, plus anything to avoid scurvy." He lifted up his fork and speared one of the strawberries.

"I wish we had some oranges or even some kiwis." Alex bit into his strawberry and savored the sweetness. "We could head to Monterey Bay. Go into Moss Landing and see if we can find anything there. That's one good thing about the coast, there are a lot of old farms."

"Seriously?" Jacob beamed. He hadn't looked this excited in a long time.

Alex couldn't help but smile. "Well, we can check things out, see what, if anything, is happening, scope it out for a day or two."

"That would be amazing."

If Jacob's smile could've gotten any larger, Alex didn't know how. "It's been, what, two months?"

"Four." Jacob countered as he bit into another strawberry and chewed slowly.

"Really? Wow." Had that much time really passed? Had they been away from the shore for four months? That didn't seem right. That would've meant they were in July... could it really be July? Alex reflected a moment on their last time venturing ashore.

This time they would need to be even more careful. They didn't have guns, unfortunately, but they had some pretty impressive knives and small daggers they had managed to get before they headed to sea. If only they had more time to prepare and more time to outfit the boat... yes, they did a darn good job. They had most of the things they needed and they managed to pull a lot of items together like the daggers, medical supplies, and books. They even managed a final large-scale trip to Costco before the National Guard came in and money became all but worthless.

How quickly everything fell apart.

He figured they were better prepared than most people, but still, they could have really used some guns. The two extra cabins had been filled with storage of the things they needed; he counted them lucky. Despite that, they had already burned through a lot of their initial supplies, no matter how good Jacob was at managing their provisions.

"We should make a list of all the things we need and all the things we'd like to get," Alex offered. He loved making lists and planning. Doing so made him feel like he had control. Like he had power over something that was so utterly out of his command.

Maybe that's why I loved commercial real estate so much.

"I'd love to get some crabbing nets or something like that." Jacob put his fork down. "I don't know if we could find some sewing supplies, but if we can, that would be helpful. I could repair the sails and fix some of our clothes. You know, I wish I would've thought of that before." Jacob sighed. "And if we could find honey, butter, and milk, even dehydrated..." Jacob licked his lips as he finished off his strawberries and began plucking out the few remaining seeds left on the bits he didn't quite eat by the stem.

Alex laughed.

"It could happen," Jacob protested.

"I'll grant you finding honey, or a cow, might be possible—or even a goat—but getting milk and butter..." Alex shook his head.

"Well, I can make butter. It's not hard, if we find a cow or goat. Really, we could use any dry goods we can find; salt and flour would be amazing."

"It would be nice to get some red meat," Alex conceded. "How long has it been since we've had actual hamburgers? Or steak?"

"What about some chickens? For the eggs."

"How would we care for them? This is only a sixty-foot boat." Alex held up a hand as the reality of their current situation rocked their little boat. "And don't say a raft."

"Fine," Jacob huffed as his eyes lit up. "What about getting a smaller boat? Something we could have alongside us and tow?"

Alex knew better than to say no outright, so he took a breath, then faced Jacob and nodded. "Maybe."

Jacob clapped his hands.

"But it'd have to be a lot smaller and something we'd be willing to cut free if the weather turned."

"If it means getting a couple of chickens and a goat, then I'm all for it."

When did I agree to a goat and chickens?

"But I'm still not sure how we would feed and care for them. We can just about support ourselves, but even small animals require a lot of fresh water and food."

"We could harvest seaweed, and we have all of our food scraps." Jacob considered. "There is a lot we could still pull from the water..."

"Look." Alex raised a hand. "Let's not get our hopes up. I doubt we'll find anything like that anyway, but we might." He leaned back on the bench seat, rubbing his chin. "I'll be happy to find some fresh veggies and fruit and anything dried. There still might be some dried goods around if they haven't already been found or used up." He met Jacob's gaze, forcing a smile to his lips. "You remember when we'd drive down to Monterey and spend the day, then stop on the way home at the local farms and pick up all kinds of stuff: fruit, artichokes, nuts. All that?"

"And you would always get your chocolate-covered raisins or pretzels."

"What I wouldn't give for some of that right now..."

"I miss chocolate." Jacob peered around the salon. "I miss being able to go to the store and buy whatever we wanted and cook whatever we fancied." His smile faded as tears started to spill from his eyes. "How did we let all this happen? Why couldn't we have been better, or done better?"

Alex moved over to him and wrapped an arm over his shoulder. "Hey. Hey, it's okay. A lot of people tried. There was more good in the world than we give credit for."

"And it wasn't enough." Jacob's voice shook. "Look how things ended up. Look where we are now."

"The world hasn't ended yet." Alex squeezed Jacob tight. "There's always hope."

"*Hope!*" Jacob snorted out a laugh. "How long are we gonna be able to live like this? Live in this boat? We're stuck together and there is no one else. We haven't seen anyone in ages."

"We don't know that. There might be others." Alex tried to sound hopeful, but Jacob was putting words to all his fears and worries.

"We haven't seen anyone in eight months, and the Navy broadcast hasn't changed in six months. There is no one here. They're all gone." Jacob wiped at his eyes. "Maybe we should go down to Catalina like the broadcast said. Maybe it'll be safe there. The Pacific Fleet was in San

Diego, and there were all the submarines and other ships, bigger ships. Maybe they're there, or maybe they all moved south."

"Maybe." Alex agreed. "And maybe it'll be like Alcatraz or Treasure Island. Those were supposed to be safe too. They destroyed the Bay Bridge on both ends and, still, it wasn't safe."

"But you don't know. We haven't been there. Catalina could be safe, the Navy and the Government said –"

"They all said a lot of things. They said Hawaii was gonna be a safe zone and Puerto Rico, but we saw what happened there before the TV and Internet stopped working. You have the luxury of having faith in the government. But no –"

"Don't!" Jacob's voice rose as his gaze snapped to meet Alex's. "Don't you play the race card with me. Never with me. I know how tough you had it, and I know how the world sees you. I can't say I understand, and I never experienced what you did, but you don't have the right to say that to me, not after all we've been through, even before the world fell to shit."

"You're right. I'm sorry." Alex adjusted his glasses and took a breath. "Given all that's happened, I don't think anything will be different."

"But we know more now," Jacob protested through tearful eyes. "This isn't like when everything started to happen. Even before we lost the TV and the Internet, there were already reports of things –"

"Do we?" Alex's words came out harder than he wanted them to be, but he remembered seeing Honolulu in flames and then San Juan going silent only a few days later. No, they didn't know, but if there was something more, they would have heard or seen something by now. Even if there was safety to be found in other countries–Brazil, Australia, South Africa, France, Japan, China, Russia–but there was nothing. They hadn't seen a plane since the FAA grounded all flights. Even the military jets and helicopters hadn't been seen in... well... a year?

"What about the rest of the world?" Jacob asked. "What about Mexico or Canada? The islands in the Caribbean? There are hundreds, if not thousands, of places we could go," He offered through his soft sobs. "I don't want to die on this boat."

Alex squeezed Jacob as tight as he could. What could he say? Thinking long term wasn't an option; he could think a week or two out. That was as far as he was willing to plan. They could arrange to visit places on the West Coast, but then what? He didn't think he could sail them to Hawaii. Yes, there were rumors, back when there were still enough people to spread them, that Japan was a safe place. They had said the same thing about New Zealand and even places like Cuba, Taiwan, and the Philippines, but how could he get them there? Crossing the ocean, the Pacific Ocean, even in the best of times, was dangerous. Luckily the satellites were still working, and they had their GPS system, but for how much longer? And they would need fuel for the engine. The few solar panels were enough to charge the boat's batteries, but for something like that, they'd need diesel, and he didn't even know if stored diesel would be any good. He remembered reading something that diesel, or maybe, gasoline, was only good for six months before it went bad.

Who would've thought diesel and gasoline could spoil, but it does. Who knew?

Alex raked a hand through his hair.

Had he missed their opportunity out of his own fear and his own self-doubt? He wasn't a sailor, not a true sailor. Yes, he spent a lot of time on sailboats and racing craft, but he wasn't a real sailor, not like his old mentors. There was a lot he wasn't sure about. Buying the *Seaduction* had a huge learning curve, one he was still discovering today.

What a stupid name; Seaduction, but Jacob thought the name was funny. Who was I to argue?

Before all hell broke loose, they had only been out day sailing with a few weekend trips here and there. Alex and Jacob hadn't gone on any long voyages because he still wanted to break in the boat and learn her. They were never far from land or a call to the Coast Guard should they need help. The boat, for all intents and purposes, was still new to him. Plus, they had their friends with them so there were enough hands to help do all the work. How could Jacob possibly believe he could traverse the Ocean and get them some place safe?

I've been lucky enough to keep this thing floating with the two of us. For something like that, we'd need more people.

Alex took a breath and pushed away all his doubt and worry. "Jacob, sweetness, we're not going to die on this boat. I'm doing –"

"You're doing nothing." Jacob snapped. "We sail up and down the coast, not close enough to be seen but close enough in case something happens." He pulled away and swiped at his eyes. "Months ago, I wanted to try and go to Hawaii, when it... and now we could go to Catalina and you won't even consider the idea. There're two big islands down there and we could –"

"And they are right off the coast of one of the largest population centers on the West Coast of the United States." Heat filled Alex's face. "How many people with a boat do you think went to Catalina? How many of the wrong people do you think got in, before they knew? How much of a shit show do you think we'll be walking into if we sail down there, and worse, what if the people aren't welcoming and want to hurt us? When the world ends, people only look after themselves, and since we're both older gay men, one of whom happens to be Black, I doubt we're on anyone's welcome list, especially since we don't have much to offer."

"We have a lot to offer," Jacob insisted.

"I did commercial real estate, and you worked for the county. I doubt they need anyone like us."

"You're an experienced sailor; you grew up on racing and sailboats. I've learned about water filtration and purification and agriculture. Plus, I've learned a lot about sea life and what resources we can pull from the sea."

"All from books." Alex pointed to the book lying on the sofa by the navigation station.

"Yes, all from books and putting what I've read to practical use here on our boat." Jacob glanced in the direction of the book he had been reading.

"They would sooner kill us and take what we have." Alex leaned his head back and faced the top of the cabin as his words grew softer. "You give people too much credit." The words were barely a whisper.

"And you don't give people any or enough credit."

"Right now, we don't have the luxury of giving people the benefit of the doubt. Our world was a divided mess before everything went to hell. Do you really think it's gotten any better?"

"I can't do this with you right now." Jacob stood and cleared his plate. "I'm going to bed, and I'd like to sleep by myself, please." He put the food scraps in the bucket they used for the plants, placed his dish and utensils in the sink, and moved across the salon to their cabin. He stopped and turned to face Alex. "Just so you know, today happens to be the Fourth of July. I kept the strawberries as a special treat for the holiday... I know you forgot, because, why would you remember?" He stepped through the cabin door and closed it behind him.

"The Fourth of July," Alex muttered to himself as he glanced down at his unfinished strawberries. Jacob continually tried to keep their spirits up, planning special things for the major holidays. It was nothing like what he did before, but he always had that carefree and spontaneous nature about him. It was part of why Alex loved him. They complimented each other so well, but now... now all they seemed to do was bicker and fight. Even when that was the last thing he—well, hopefully, either of them—wanted to do.

He played with the few strawberries he still had and, instead of tossing them like he would have in the olden times, he grabbed a towel and slowly picked out the strawberry seeds one at a time. He knew that Jacob could germinate the seeds and plant them for more strawberries. Jacob typically took care of the plants and ensured they had seeds to work with. It was one of the many thankless jobs Jacob did around the boat. Yes, Alex kept the yacht functioning and secure, but Jacob took care of the rest.

Alex glanced around the interior of the boat. Everything was put away, organized, and tidy. If Jacob had all the cleaning supplies he wanted, Alex was sure the whole boat would sparkle like new. It wasn't easy maintaining a boat with all the saltwater and salt in the air, yet Jacob managed a lot.

Alex ran a hand through his hair. Another thing he missed was going to the barber shop. He sighed as he fussed with his glasses. The sound of the waves lapping against the boat was the only noise that made way to his ears.

After cleaning up and ensuring the seeds were secure with the other seeds that Jacob collected, Alex crossed over to the navigation station. He picked up Jacob's book, *The Encyclopedia of Country Living*, and smiled. Jacob really had been learning a lot more than Alex gave him credit for. He placed the book to the side and started going through all the navigation charts he had, doing his best to plot out a course. They could make their way to Catalina after stopping in Monterey, getting what they can there. See about finding a smaller boat they could secure to their boat and maybe even see about getting some small animals like chickens and a goat or two.

It's probably a dream, but one worth trying for.

Alex reviewed the charts and, given today was apparently July fourth, they might be able to head out to Hawaii. In theory, the weather should be good and, again, in theory, they could make the trip in three weeks, maybe four. The one thing Jacob forgets is that he's only one person and, yes, he does okay sailing this boat up and down the west coast, but for a journey across the ocean, they needed a crew of at least four or five, and even with Jacob's full help, they don't currently have enough hands.

It's not that I don't want to try, I just don't see how we can make or survive such a journey. Especially with no one around to help, or save, us.

Alex pulled off his glasses and pinched the bridge of his nose. Was trying for Hawaii or somewhere even farther worth the effort? They could go south, see what they can see. Learn what they can. He would need to push Jacob, teach him and get him involved with all aspects of sailing. They couldn't take on something like a trip to Hawaii without at least Jacob's help, if they can't find one or two more people. It was a risk.

But Jacob's right: I don't want to die on this boat. I don't want to die without trying.

By the next morning, Alex had convinced himself that Jacob had a point, and they should at least try. Sleep hadn't come easy, but Alex felt better than he had in months. This new sense of purpose was perhaps the kick in the ass he needed. So, he pulled a very basic breakfast together and made his way to the cabin where Jacob had vanished off to. He knocked on the door and opened it slowly.

"May I come in?" Alex asked, holding a plate in one hand.

"Here to tell me how everything is going to be all right?" Jacob snapped. "How we're safe where we are and don't need anyone else?"

"No." Alex's voice played out level and calm. "I brought you breakfast. It's nothing special, but I did my best."

Jacob shifted on the bed, a partial smile blooming over his lips.

When they bought the sailboat, it was a lot of creams and whites. The old owners didn't make any changes to the décor, and the color scheme did make the space appear bigger and more open than it really was. However, Jacob spent a lot of time and money making the cabin and the whole inside of the boat reflect them and their personalities. The wood tones were kept the same, but he brought in blues to the room, making the space cool and look like they were floating in a cloud. Alex really loved all the touches Jacob added throughout the boat.

"I can't believe you cooked."

"Well, not so much cooking as pulling things together." Alex placed the plate down for Jacob to take and sat next to him. "I did some thinking and some planning and here's my thought. We go to Monterey Bay to see what we can see and get what we can..." Alex held up his hand to Jacob, cutting off any comments. "Then we head down the coast to Catalina. However, during that time, you're going to have to step up and we're really going to need to work as a team on handling this boat, and I'm going to have to help you with all the other work, because we're in this together and we need to work together to survive... and hopefully thrive. We need each other on this ship."

"Boat." Jacob smirked.

Alex bit back his smile. "I know you think I keep us close to land because I'm afraid, and that's partly true. This is a big boat–and requires more hands than we have–and I want to ensure if something goes wrong, we have a place to retreat to using the dinghy. If we want to make a try for Hawaii and other places that may be safe, it's going to take the two of us, and even then..."

"Anything." Jacob nodded. "I know you do a lot and keep us sailing and if that means I have to do more, I will. I'm scared of doing something wrong and making things worse. I know you said ruining the first sail wasn't my fault, but if I had been better, knew more... If we could find sewing supplies, I know I could repair it and we'd have a backup again. I can't let you down again."

"You never let me down, ever, not once. Not during this entire time." Alex pulled off his glasses. "I think we both feel like we let each other down a lot."

Jacob bit at his lower lip.

"And my other thought is that maybe, if we can find one or two more people–I'm not saying we will, but we can try–then we might be able to make a real go of it. Either way, I think we should head to Hawaii while the weather is good and while we still have our navigation and GPS."

"Thank you," Jacob leaned closer to Alex. "I think we can do this."

"At least we're going to try." Alex kissed the top of Jacob's head before standing up, "Now finish your breakfast and make your way up on deck. You've got a lot to learn, and we need to start heading to Monterey."

"Yes, Captain."

"Don't call me that." Alex smiled. "Well, maybe when we're in bed." He raised his eyebrows and walked out of the cabin.

Well, here goes everything.

The day moved swiftly and, much to Alex's surprise and relief, Jacob was a faster study than he thought. Perhaps during all this time, he was paying attention and absorbing the work. Sure, there were things–a lot of things–he needed to learn, but he was getting there and they might actually have a better chance at making the trip than he thought.

After dinner and as night fell, the wind began to pick up. The once calm sea turned choppy, and dark clouds loomed on the horizon. Alex inhaled. They weren't too far from Monterey Bay, but with a storm coming, they would be more exposed than he hoped. They might be able to ride the bad weather closer to Moss Landing, but none of it was ideal and bad weather always made Alex worry. "Looks like a storm is brewing, maybe the remains of a hurricane from Mexico," Alex said, his tone more a question than a statement, and his voice tinged with concern.

Jacob raised a hand to his head, looking out at the sea and the growing clouds. "We've handled worse together. I'm sure between us, we've got this. After all, I wanna tan my fat ass off the coast of Hawaii in a month."

Qalam Bal

Wayne Goodman

"You must come to Barcelona," Ishmael wrote in his letter. "You can compete here without fear."

A few years before receiving that invitation, I had written to the Municipal Records in Barcelona to continue some family research. The person who responded informed me that most of the records for Jews had been destroyed over time but that he would look into the matter and let me know what he had found.

When Ishmael wrote again, he confirmed that any formal government records of my family's existence could not be located. However, his ancestors had arrived in Barcelona as part of the Moorish invasion and never left. He would speak to some of his older family members and ask if they had any information.

He also seemed curious about Boston, where I lived. Cradle of the American Revolution. Cultural hub. How much I loved living in one of his favorite cities.

His curiosity shifted to subjects like art and baseball. Then he started asking more questions about me, my family, and what I enjoyed. I'm not sure what he read into my responses, but after a few letters back and forth, it felt like Ishmael had more interest in me than in Boston or finding my family records.

Then he sent a photo. I had to assume it was him. It showed an olive-skinned fellow about my age with slicked back, jet black hair. The gaze from his caramel eyes stared right through me. I shuddered and felt a quickening in my chest.

I included a shot of me in my next letter. That took quite a bit of courage. I never considered myself worth looking at, with my curly, rusty red hair, a pasty face full of freckles, and a *schnozz* like a camel. Perhaps his tastes included unusual-looking people like me.

As a poor, lanky, Jewish kid from Dorchester, I never fit in with the others my age. When I reached high school, I discovered track and field, specifically sprinting. My gawky physique allowed me to outrun any of those muscly lads. One day, as I crossed the finish line a full second ahead of my nearest competitor, I threw my pencil-like arms in the air and waggled my hands a few times. This became my signature move when I won races, which happened every time I competed.

When I reached 18, my coach suggested training for the upcoming Olympic Games in Berlin. I ran every day, getting my sprint times down as far as I could. Every hundredth of a second motivated me to push harder and harder.

My parents worried that sending me into the jaws of the National Socialist Party would be my doom. I had read their leader first banned Jews and Negroes from competing, but, after political pressure, relented. The German team would include a half-Jewish woman swimmer.

Correspondence from overseas continued to grace our postbox, and one day my mother inquired, "What's with all these letters from *Spain*?" as she handed me the latest letter. Her squinty, sidelong expression suggested suspicions I did not want to address.

"Um... I've been doing research on our family," was the only thing I could think of. At least, that's how it started.

One of her eyebrows arched. "Oh, have you found anything?"

I wanted to shout, "Love!" but I worried my mother would not understand the feelings her only child had developed for a *goyishe* foreigner through letter writing. Whenever I stood anywhere near her, I heard a clock ticking down time to the arrival of her grandchildren.

"Not yet," I informed her. "But my friend in Barcelona tells me he will keep looking."

As the conversation with Ishmael intensified, he began referring to me as "Qalam Bal," which he said meant "pen pal," but his frequent use of it suggested a deeper meaning than just friends across the water.

When I wrote and told him about my Olympic ambitions, he responded that Barcelona would be a better choice. The city had been a finalist for the 1936 games, but the international committee decided on the German capital instead. In opposition to the political and ethical upheavals of the time, the new Spanish Republican government withdrew from the global competition and decided to host its own "People's Olympiad," where everyone could compete, regardless of national origin or religion.

Without the threat of anti-Zionism, participating in Barcelona sounded very attractive. And, I would get to meet Ishmael in person.

When I discussed this option with my parents, I could see their relief as tense shoulders lowered and smiles appeared. They told me they would finance my trip, but if I brought any medals home, they would become family heirlooms.

I wrote to my Qalam Bal, informing him of my plans. His response: "I cannot wait to be together with you. Come a week early so that I can show you around my precious Barcelona. You would have to stay with me because there aren't enough hotel rooms to board all the visiting athletes."

That sounded good to me, and it would lower the cost to my folks.

My anxiety about meeting Ishmael outpaced anticipation of the competition. I pictured his handsome face in my mind throughout the day. His letters became the emotional center of my life. I read them upon waking and fell asleep holding the latest one. They encouraged me that his interest in me matched mine in him.

The only other boy I had ever been with was a fellow named Lenny whom I met at Hebrew school. He had wavy chestnut hair and the most beautiful eyelashes. A very talented fellow who sang and played piano for our congregation.

One day our teacher did not show up to class and the cantor dismissed us. Rather than go home, Lenny led me to a secluded area under some trees in a nearby park. We kissed and rubbed each other's crotches through our trousers. I made a mess in mine, but he never did.

My parents put me on a ship sailing to the Mediterranean. Mom gave me long kisses and even longer hugs. When the whistle blew, they walked away waving and cheering.

The crossing took four days, and I ran around the deck as much as possible to keep up my training. Many of the other competitors were Jews headed to the Olympiad as well. At Marseille I took an overnight train to Barcelona.

Ishmael met me at Sants station with something that looked like a cross between a wobbly bicycle and a rickety motorbike. It had two seats, but I lacked confidence in its ability to transport us anywhere safely.

"Qalam Bal!" Ishmael shouted with open arms for a long-awaited hug. I started to tear up when the intimacy lasted longer than the second or two I anticipated.

I stepped back, dropped my rucksack, and grasped both his wrists. "Ishmael," I croaked. He looked even better in person. The golden Spanish sunlight added a warm glow to his skin. The smile alone claimed me in an instant, and all thoughts of precarious vehicles vanished like parting fog.

"It is so good to see you in person," he warbled, eyeing me up and down. His musical tenor voice sounded even more enticing than Benny Goodman's clarinet. "Much better than that little photo you sent." A sly grin crossed his face.

Not knowing how to respond, I went with, "And you look really good as well." I think I smiled. I can't remember, but I know I had never been happier.

His English sounded much like the announcers I listened to on the BBC Empire Radio News. "How many languages do you speak?"

He cocked his head. "Ummm... Spanish, English, some Arabic, Catalan..."

"That's pretty impressive," I admitted. Back in the States, all I ever used was English. American style.

"Hop on!" he ordered, stepping over the bike's chassis.

"What is *that*?" I squawked, pointing at the thing.

"A Reynolds," he responded with a gleam of pride.

I flung a leg over one side, and he assisted me into the pillion behind him. I threw my arms in the air and waggled my hands.

Ishmael looked back and squealed, "What is *that*?"

I shrugged and parted my parched-looking lips enough to expose the slightly yellow teeth below.

He tilted his head to one side and fluttered his eyelids. "Hold on!" he commanded as he handed me the rucksack.

With pleasure.

As I clutched his torso, the flimsy cycle propelled us through the busy streets. I kept craning my neck to take in all the stately old buildings and fancy new ones. This helped me to avoid focusing on the bustling traffic he swerved between and around.

At one point we had to stop for a group of people with banners and protest signs marching ahead of us.

"What is *that*?" I inquired.

"Oh, it's another workers' strike. Ever since the new government took over, people have been organizing for better pay and conditions."

That sounded familiar. "Are they Communists?"

"They might be."

"My dad says Communists are just snakes in the grass waiting to feed on the unhappy masses." Of course, he has something negative to say about just about every group that isn't Jews. And sometimes it's Jews who disagree with him.

"Your papa sounds like a wise man. You are like him. No?"

Oh, God, I hope not.

After about a half hour of terror and delight, we stopped in front of an old apartment building. Familiar brownstone interspersed with alternating yellow and red bricks.

"This is where I live," Ishmael informed me.

He helped me off the contraption, and I felt like kissing the ground.

"You're shaking," he observed.

"Am I? Hadn't noticed."

He reached his arms around me and gave a long hug. "There. Now we are even."

"*Even!* What do you mean?"

His grin mesmerized me. "You have been holding on to me for the last thirty minutes. I wanted my chance to hold on to you."

So romantic. I could only hope this level of affection continued for the length of my stay.

He led me around the side of the building into a dim alley. "Aren't we going in?" I asked.

"This way." He pointed to a gray door that blended in with the stones around it. "No one uses the front entrance."

I followed him up seven flights of a circular staircase with black, wrought iron handrails to a door that looked like all the other doors. He opened it without a key.

"You leave your place unlocked?"

"We are all honest people here. If you lock your door, people think you have something to hide. I have nothing to hide, Qalam Bal."

He stepped in and I followed into what I would have called a bachelor apartment, one large room with a tiny bathroom off to the side. The view from the single window showed other apartments across an air shaft.

Ishmael closed the door, stepped toward me, and inquired, "Are we together now?"

It took me a second to realize the reference to an earlier letter, *I cannot wait to be together with you.* Perhaps the word had an additional meaning this time.

"Yes. I believe we are," I responded with a lump in my throat.

When we hugged face-to-face, my *putz* responded right away. I'm sure Ishmael could feel it. I pulled back, whining, "I'm sorry. I'm sorry. I'm sorry."

He embraced me, kissed my cheek, my forehead, and lips, then whispered, "You never have to be sorry about *that*."

I awoke each morning blissful and content, having spent the previous evening in the arms of a man whose affection I craved more and more.

Ishmael lived in a neighborhood known as La Bordeta, a short walk– or run–from Montjuïc Stadium. In the mornings, I would jog to the arena and practice sprinting on the track to get a good feel of the conditions so that I might have a bit of an advantage over the others.

Following my daily workout, Ishmael would putt-putt me around Barcelona, pointing out various historical sites or places with famous names, none of which I could remember later. Only La Sagrada Familia, an unfinished church designed by Antonio Gaudí, burned itself into my memory. Four tapering spires rose up to heaven. We didn't have any churches like that in Dorchester.

"All those curvy shapes," I observed. "Like something out of a creepy dream."

"That's his style. All the buildings he designed have flowing lines like that."

"Why didn't they complete it?" I asked.

"He was killed by a tram in 1926," he responded.

"Oh, but they've had ten years. You would think they could have finished it by now."

"Things move at a slower pace here in Spain. We can only hope and pray it gets done in a hundred years."

People from all over the world had begun to assemble in Barcelona for the Olympiad. As Ishmael had correctly surmised, there were not sufficient hotel rooms for the visitors, and many of them slept under the grandstands. The day before the start, we rehearsed our opening ceremony, and I got to meet others from so many countries.

Since I arrived, Ishmael has shown me nothing but kindness and intimacy. His letters encouraged my interest in him, but spending time in person has turned me into an emotional puddle. I knew my own amorous feelings, but I could only guess how he felt about me.

That night, over dinner, I confessed to Ishmael, "I think I want to move here to Barcelona to be with you."

When he stopped choking on his garlic chicken, he responded, "So soon? Don't you have to go back to the States? Won't your parents be expecting you?"

"I don't feel like I have anything to go back to. Barcelona has everything I could ever want. My parents have no idea that I prefer men and they are never getting grandchildren out of me." I lowered my chin. "I'm sorry if that came out too fast for you."

"Oh, no, Qalam Bal." He stood and moved around the table to hug me. "Not at all. I have been hoping for this outcome as well, but I thought it too presumptuous of me to mention it."

We kissed and left the chicken on the table to get cold.

The day of the opening ceremony, we walked to the stadium with wide grins. The muscles in my face hurt from so much smiling. I had never been happier.

Ishmael and I entered the arena as the visiting participants started to crawl out from under the grandstand. Thousands of us took our positions on the track to prepare for the parade.

Minutes before the first words of the opening ceremony, gunshots rang out on the streets near the stadium. We rushed under the seats to take cover.

Cries of "Paquito! Paquito!" came from the distance.

I turned to Ishmael. "What is Paquito?"

"Not what, who. That's the rebels' name for Franco. Keep your head down."

"I heard he was in Africa or the Canary Islands or some other place." One of the newspapers I had read aboard ship mentioned something about that.

Ishmael grabbed my hand and pulled me toward the exit closest to his apartment building. "Sounds like he's come back to start a revolution. We have got to get out and get away."

"Wouldn't we be safer here?" I looked at all the frightened faces as we passed through the huddled contestants.

"No. They would have us trapped. If we can make it across the Gran Via we should be fine."

Others followed us as we made our way out of the stadium. By the time we reached the street, about 100 people had joined us. Sweat streamed down my face. Some of the moisture might have been tears. My throat tightened as I felt I was going to die on foreign soil.

"This way!" Ishmael commanded as he yanked me to the left across Avenida de l'Estadi.

Hundreds of red-shirted, gun-toting rebels blocked our path. "Paquito! Paquito! *Viva la Muerte!*" They shouted as they fired dozens of rounds into our group. Bullets whizzed by my ears, and I ducked without thinking.

My accelerated breathing stopped when I saw Ishmael splayed out on the asphalt beside me. His white shirt turning red before my eyes.

"Ishmael!" Deep sobs of anguish erupted from my gullet as I bent to cuddle him in my arms.

His eyes barely open, he managed to gasp, "I love you Qalam Bal, and I always will."

Someone in the crowd grabbed my arm and pulled me away from my lover's death scene.

"No! Let me go!" I yelled as I struggled to head in the opposite direction.

"*Vamos! Vamos!*" the stranger screamed as the distance between me and Ishmael grew.

Once our crowd crossed the grand avenue, he released me. I ran back to Ishmael's place, crying and heaving all the way. Through the gray door, up seven flights of stairs, and into the unlocked apartment.

For the first time in my life, someone loved me the way I wanted to be loved. Unimportant, unattractive me. Someone I allowed myself to love in return. Gone. The Olympiad. Gone. The whole world. Gone to *drek*.

As my breathing and heart rate returned to a more normal pace, I tried to come up with a reason, any reason, to go back home. Not finding one, I decided to put our story down in these words and leave it here on the desk where Ishmael sat and wrote all those enchanting letters. I hope that someone will discover our brief love story and understand what it meant for an awkward Jewish boy from Boston to have found someone to love who loved him back.

After leaving the safety and comfort of his flat, I plan to run out into the street, arms in the air, waggling my hands, until one of the revolutionaries shoots me or I get struck down by a streetcar.

I love you, Ishmael, and I always will.

THAT INTIMACY THING

MICHAEL ALENYIKOV

Roger wants us to go away for a week. I do not. He's collected brochures for bed and breakfasts. He's maxed his Gold Visa card with its shimmering silver hologram: on camping equipment, a kite, cross country skis, and snorkeling gear. They fill his once tidy apartment, totems to Roger's simple faith in our future. Together.

Roger loves the outdoors. "For me, it's like church," he says.

Maybe if we take a trip he'll be distracted, and we won't fight.

For weeks he's been saying we're losing the intimacy thing. What's it look like, I'd say? If it's a thing, what's its shape, its color, its size? Where'd we leave it? I'd ask, egging him on, imagining something warm to the touch, soft like velvet, bordello red and sticky with Velcro; too large to misplace in a drawer or closet; too obvious of value to throw out by mistake with the trash.

"Let's go somewhere, *anywhere*," he coos, ignoring my taunts, licking the inside of my ear. "Let's do something totally dorky, like go to the Poconos."

"No way," I say, "It's too cold. And, besides, I want to stay home and read, in bed, with you."

"We'll watch *The Bitter Tears of Petra Von Kant* again. You know we will," he says and holds his hands out towards me, palms up, like a supplicating saint, eagerness and innocence stamped on his face.

I'm drowning in him and wonder: is the same as love?

I can't say for sure how we decided to go fly a kite on Fire Island: a day trip, an edgy compromise.

We set out on an oddly warm December Saturday. The sun, a pale winter disk with the look of a communion wafer, hugs the horizon, early in its low winter arc across the sky. A twitchy Citibank sign reads seventy degrees. Nervous euphoria unsettles the faces of people on the street. It's expressed in tentative smiles and furtive glances; a conspiracy of unspoken hope that this year winter might never arrive, leavened with a wariness of being taken in, of being made fools of once again.

We walk along East 7th Street towards Avenue A. I follow Roger, whose long loping strides gather such momentum I think he might take flight. The image of a giraffe with wings, a mutant angel, one of god's sillier failed experiments, takes shape in my mind. The red and black Chinese dragon kite dances behind him.

On Avenue A Roger hails a cab and we stuff ourselves into the smell of synthetic pine cones. Roger says to the cabby, "Penn Station," and I say to Roger, "We could have walked." Without turning his head to look at me he says, "This is just great, don't worry."

I say, "Oh really?" and struggle to remember some detail I love about him: the feel of our legs entwined in bed; the way when I'm lonely, he'd startle me with an unexpected touch; the steady rhythmic sound of his breathing while he slept, a silky thread that, lying awake at night, I'd follow, thinking it would lead me to some safe, secure place, whose terrain I'd imagined he knew far better than me.

The ferry to the Island is half full; men, mostly, with fading tans and perfect haircuts. In the austere winter light, I conjure ghosts, and the boat feels haunted. Roger's dark-tinted glasses mask his eyes. I can see my reflection: small, distant, like looking the wrong way through binoculars, and queasy doubts seep into me with the wind's damp salty spray.

On the dock we hop off and follow the smell of salt and sea to the beach. Solitary men with sculpted chests, each identical, stroll past. Roger and I love the beach but we're not Fire Island types. Our modest pecs are square enough, but there's a lack of precision, a lack of rigor to our cooking and place settings, our clothes, our careers and, I'd always assumed, to our clunky and passionate love making. For the first time I wonder if Roger made love differently with the men he was with before me. I take his hand. He gives me a puzzled look. Until now, it had been his job to take *my* hand, to reassure.

The beach is empty. Walking along the water's edge with Roger and our kite, my mood improves. We make sense, yes, we do; the whole *is* greater than the sum of its parts. We could live together; we *could* be happy.

Roger runs along the beach with the kite. Sand flies out from beneath his feet. I struggle to keep up. The kite gains height, then falls. But Roger, patient in a way I could never be, yanks purposefully on the string. The kite bounces in the air but each time the wind fails it.

"Let me try," I say, but he shakes me off. His patience, I'm reminded, is built when I least expect it, on a headstrong determination to go it alone. Finally, with Roger dancing on his toes, wind and speed take the kite aloft. He runs in loops and circles, hooting and hollering, his face, a drunken smile of joy. The kite soars ever higher, a small dark speck, mingling with the heavens.

Roger seems to offer me the string but doesn't completely let go and for a moment we're both pulling on the line.

"Let go," I say tersely, and he does. Roger says he wants to live with me, that he needs me, but when I watch him at times like these, he seems to be in his own private playground and I realize how much like a prop I feel, like I could be anyone, that he could come alive as easily in the eyes of any other man.

The kite suddenly dips. I pull on the string to gain control but it snaps and bucks in the wind. Roger grabs my hand roughly. "For Chrissake, give it some slack. Let it fly. Let it fly free," he says, tightening his grip on my hand until I shake him off. "You hold on to everything too tight, that's your problem," he says. "Sometimes I can't feel myself breathe when I'm with you." His forehead and mouth tighten in anger. I step backward, my feet and calves slapped by the cold surf, and watch as the anger becomes rage, which sweeps across his face with the abruptness of a flash flood. When it subsides he looks sheepish, startled at his own intensity

Hurt and confused, I wonder: why does he want to live with me if I'm so suffocating?

We walk along the shore. The kite trails aimlessly behind me. The silence deepens recklessly. I feel connected to Roger by an invisible rope, one end knotted in my stomach the other in his; the knots pulling on our guts.

I don't know what he wants; what I don't want is this.

The clouds have become thicker, more deeply gray; in the distance, a soft rumble. Roger trips on a piece of driftwood and stumbles, breaking his fall with his hands. I look away, embarrassed by this revelation of his newfound clumsiness.

Suddenly, he tugs on my shirt.

"Enough kites for one day," he says. The old Roger is back, and he slips the string from my hand into his. "Let this one go free," he whoops, jumping up and down. The kite hovers indecisively in the wind, then turns its back on us and is sucked up into the sky.

"Let's do it in the dunes," he says and next, hidden by some bushes, we're rolling in the sand like it's real summer, not this faux stuff. "We've never made love outdoors," he says as he slides my shirt off. "And it *is* our ninth anniversary," he adds, unbuckling my belt.

"Nine months," we cry in unison as I roll him over on his stomach and separate him from his clothes. Then, beginning with the toes of his left foot, I run my tongue the length of his long skinny body avoiding the patches of light and dark crusted sand that have stuck to his skin. He tastes of sweat: oily, pungent, salty like sardines.

When I reach the back of his neck he flips over and grips my head in his hands. "We could live together, you know, like an experiment," he says, and I imagine a mad scientist's laboratory with foaming vials. "We can always be roommates if it doesn't work out," he adds, a touch of pleading in his voice.

"You sound desperate," I say and feel cruel. Our arms and legs become entangled like a pretzel and I try to feel where exactly I begin and Roger leaves off. In the process of searching one of us lets go and we fall apart.

He lays his face on my lap and sucks like a child, then stops and looks up. "I want you inside of me," he says, softly. He reaches for his pants, digs into a pocket, then hands me a rubber. This is the first time Roger has let me fuck him.

Inside of him now, I am in love: with his smooth sweaty back, the shape of his butt, the hair on his thin legs that ends abruptly midway up each thigh, like a line of showers in a distant spring storm. I can feel Roger's doubt; about me, about us, and that feeling is exhilarating.

"I love the nape of your neck," I whisper in his ear, and he turns his head to say, "Slower, you're hurting me."

Then he rolls us over and I'm looking into his eyes. "I need to know soon," he says.

"Know what?"

"Whether you want to live with me."

I start to pull out. "Don't," he says with a whimper that shocks me with its nakedness. "I need to know, I just do," he says; and, as if in reply to his question, feeling his warm, uneven breath on my neck, his hands clutching, slipping, searching my back for patches of sand and mud, for traction, I sink even more deeply into him.

Moments later, Roger comes with a long sigh and a smooth hum; I follow, sputtering like an old Chevy. The wind rustles crackling ferns and scraggly grasses, blowing sand into darting whirlwinds around us. Rain begins to fall, a steady drumbeat of large, warm, wet drops, landing on sand, on skin: the sounds of intimacy, so close.

First published under the name Michael Stuart Allen in *Modern Words: A thoroughly queer literary journal*, under the title "Communion."

SELECTED POETRY

SARAH WHITE

PREFACE

Dear Reader,

In the tangled corridors of the heart, where passions intertwine and emotions collide, there exists a sacred trinity of love, each unique, each profound, each bearing the weight of its tumultuous journey. Welcome, Reader, to a realm where poetry and prose become the vessel for unyielding forces of love, where words dance upon the precipice of ecstasy and despair, and where the human soul bared itself in raw vulnerability all in the name of being "Together!"

Within these pages, I invite you to join me on a voyage through the depths of three fictional and distinct queer women's love stories and tragic endings; a journey illuminated by the flickering limerence with masterminding, the haunting echoes of sitting with the demons of infidelity, and the reverent celebration of sacred love prayers answered. Here, we shall traverse the landscapes of passion and pain, of joy and sorrow, delving into the very essence of what it means to be "Together" in the chaotic symphony of partnership, emphasis on chaos.

In the first poem, dedicated to Meredith, journey through the tangled emotions of falling for a lover so deeply that you're willing to rewrite your very essence. Feel the rawness of vulnerability, the ache of sacrifices made, and the flickers of hope that light the path of a love that demands everything. It's about the complications, the pain, and the undying belief that this love, tumultuous and transformative, is worth every change and every moment of heartache.

In the second poem, consecrated to Whitney, is a journey through the demons and consequences of infidelity, unraveling a "Together" that was once sacred but got washed away by another woman's lips. It's about not truly understanding the depths and meaning of being "Together" with the one you truly love until that bond was shattered by the cruel decision of betrayal. Feel the heartache of realizing too late what it meant to hold onto a love so profound, only to watch it crumble under the weight of broken trust and lost promises.

And finally, in the third poem, is devoted to Mandoline. This is a love letter to Mandoline and to love itself, to inclusion, to bliss, to the sweet taste of perfection, where wholeness is found in each other's arms. It's the cheesy love we've all dreamed of and aspire to hold–a "Together" so profound that simply reading about it fills your heart with butterflies. It's about the magic of finding that one person who completes you, turning everyday moments into a symphony of joy and contentment. Here's to a love so deep, so true, that it makes you believe in fairytales again.

So, dearest reader, I bid you embark upon this odyssey of the heart, where the essence of love and "Together" is laid bare in all its complexity and beauty. May these poems serve as a beacon of light amidst the darkness of your turbulent seas of emotion and awaken within you a deeper understanding of different eras of being "Together."

MEREDITH

I am wildly in love with you
And it is fucking up my life
I stare out my window, formulating being together every midnight
Every breath feels like wear and tear on my lifeline
But how strongly my heart feels this love happens once in a hundred
    lifetimes
But how the chemistry between us hits me like a fine Napa red wine
I'm guilty of iniquity; I'm masterminding how to be together again
Oh, Meredith, how I wish you had never met me
Oh, Meredith, how I wish we weren't evidence of an alchemy
I assure you that I wear my heart right on my sleeve
When it's convenient, you assure me your heart is still reserved for me
You dangle we're not official, but say we're on a winning streak
Meredith, you're the only trophy I'd cheat to win
So, I lay awake every night to crack open your locks
Willing to change all of me
Throwing my unabridged essence away
Throw it at wild cayotes or at Cliff House's rocks

Will tomorrow you say you love me
Will tomorrow I be enough
Will tomorrow you genuinely reach for my hand
And I can toss away these handcuffs

Your touch, a whisper upon my skin
Sending a shiver down where passion begins
The way my T-shirt wrinkles when you pull me in
Blood rushes to my cheeks, turning it a sultry shade of maroon
As your gentle hand pushes my hair away
You nuzzle your tender lips to my neck, where our secrets play
I come back into my body as I see you look away
Stupid girl, "We're only friends."
Her actions talk, Miss Lovestruck. Turn the volume all the way up
All these fatal fantasies, oh, what a ruthless way to die
I stare out these shattered windows, casting storms in my eyes

My heart, my body, my trust, my touch
Every inch of my being I offered up
Yet, for her, it's still not enough
Now I'm searching for haunting signs not to give up
So, I plot, I plan, I scheme, I twist
I mold myself into a shape that just might fit
I'm a façade to match your elegantly painted view
Hoping tomorrow I am finally enough to win you
Everyday I shrink more in size
And I accept that's my fate if you're the love my life

Will tomorrow you say you love me
Will tomorrow I be enough
Will tomorrow you genuinely reach for my hand
And I can toss away these handcuffs

Am I praying to the wrong, false God
Or not trying hard enough to stir fate
What if I rolled out the tempests of our differences and your hesitations
    away
Would you finally say what I have been wanting to hear for so long
That we are together, under the same moon, the same stars, the same sun
Hand in hand, in no more darkened secret rooms, we are one
Help me change my form to fit the shape of your life
Make every ounce of me fit into your creases and folds just right
My friends say it shouldn't be like this; myself, the incurable sacrifice
But I say it's what you have to do to be together with the love of your life
They don't know how you take off all my clothes and kiss me until I am
    senseless
They don't know how you touch me in ways I never felt ever before or
    ever since
So, when you leave me to my vices all alone
I slide down the wall and gently caress my collarbone
And I trace your initials on my upper thighs
Prying neighbors hear my feminine rose moan then sigh
As I fantasize about your lips, I crave to call only mine

Will tomorrow you say you love me
Will tomorrow I be enough

Will tomorrow you genuinely reach for my hand
And I can toss away these handcuffs
Ricocheted tears crash onto my pillow as my broken heart beats in sin
Isn't that the way these nights without you always end
Being together shouldn't come with such a life-altering expense
But I empty my pockets, I put all my cards out on the table
"Check, please!" The price of being yours, I'll pay.
I will give up all that makes me if you confess we are twin flames
I'm mindlessly dreaming of calculated Checkmates
Forever stuck in a Lover's Chess Game
But Babe, how can we win when you change the rules every day
Fuck all the naysayers, dream crushers, and myth busters
What do they know about us anyway

Will tomorrow you say you love me
Will tomorrow I be enough
Will tomorrow you genuinely reach for my hand
And I can toss away these handcuffs

It's 4 AM, I lay awake with your memory over me
Your love's taunting me, teasing me, how being together would be
What a real fucking legacy we would be to leave
This crumbling town, where all the beating hearts say we'll be together
    any day now
I'm endlessly obsessing with the art of calculation's guise
I'd spend forever molding my essence to fit your skies
Dreaming how I can build a bridge to your rogue sea
With every premeditated move, every clandestine scheme
Lost in the labyrinth of becoming together with
Cemented handprints of you and me.
I can keep watering my flourishing limerence
Or lay here in a pool of my fate-torn blood
Until we are truly together, it will make no difference

Will tomorrow you say you love me
Will tomorrow I be enough
Will tomorrow you genuinely reach for my hand
And I toss away these handcuffs

I'm crying in my prayers, screaming, "But Mommy, I love her!"
I'm swinging for the fences, taking my chances every damn hour
Trying to be together with wedded rings forever
My bones ache for you
My soul stays awake for you
In these lovesick bedsheets, I beckon you
To want me like I do you
And to call my hips home
But answered prayers are far and few in between
So, I swirl my dreams of you into my poems
On my diary's paper, my ink bleeds
Of hopes and dreams of my loving you schemes
So, let the heavens tremble and sever
I am the wreckage of my own endeavors
I'll tear apart the tapestry of my own being
On my knees, pissed off, heart bleeding
Hands covering my face, please, babe, I'm pleading
Grab my hand while I have a pulse for you
Before this good love starts seizing
Meredith, I'd drown for your love in oceans so deep
Where our shadows dance and our secrets keep
So, call me your sweetheart; call me your baby
Please act like you more than tolerate me
You know I can't love those bedroom eyes of anyone else
But the worst part of it all is you **know damn well**
That for you, I would ruin myself
Just to be together.

WHITNEY

Do I really have to tell you where I was on January 8th
Can't we call an ace an ace and a spade a spade?
Now, I can't stop the cascade of weeping I caused
We're both drowning in the tears rolling down your pretty face
You asked me so many times if the rumors of whose lipstick was left on
the glass was true
Now you know the secrets out, the worst thing I have ever done is what
I did to you
Whitney, this was high infidelity.
I drank her wine and made a home in her city
My secrets with her are bone deep
I danced around the truth when I dragged my feet through our door
I accused you of acting crazy when you were rightfully a woman scorned
I kept cool and calm despite our growing rift
I avoided all evidence you noticing our sinking ship
I didn't want either of you to get away
I am only to blame. I was selfish. I was corrupt
Now I sit with the consequences of the diamond rings I gave up
I thought I could keep this affair locked away in a vault
I thought I could keep my labored breath at the thought of her under
control
She'd kiss my upper thigh, playing with my mind, knowing if you knew
you would crash and die
I kept you away from this adultery maze, away from her sultry top-lip
kiss
Burying the smell of her perfume was proof I was guilty of sin.
All these winter days, you stayed home and watched the wilt of our rose
All those winter nights, I slept next to her while you slept all alone
Do I really have to tell you where I was on January 8th
Do I need to explain I saved my New Year's Kiss just for her
How I planned to talk my way out of being late again
But you always knew better
You threw blazing, daggered slurs
For months, I've been calling someone else "baby"
For months, I've been a snake dressed in sacred matrimony clothing

I got lost in her lustful transgressions, I know I went way too far this
    time
Whitney, I am what I did
The burden to carry the ashes of what was us is all mine
I broke you, our home, our love that was to stand the test of time
You told me a million times how I was the love of your life
I played with fire, and now you're the loss of my mine
It was all just so delicate
Your heart was glass, and I dropped it
It shattered into a million little pieces, I counted
I swear I loved you despite being braided next to her
We built a home together out of pure love
But I lit a match birthed from desire and watched it burn
I replay it all back, every second in my head
Sneaking from her secret room back into your bed
I can't blame you for walking out when my hands are painted red
My silent treason got the volume turned up
Now I am lovesick all over this vacant bed
I was sworn into infidelity by one single kiss, but only the first a few
    hundred times
To miss you is to love you
The opposite, trust me, I have tried
Now, there's an inconsolable ache in you because there was a selfish
    ache in me
This scarlet letter is all mine. I wear this bleeding accountability
My hands are covering my face in disbelief; miracles can't help me now
Friends whisper, "Darling, nothing lasts forever..."
But I am the one who took us down
I know we are not together now, and there is nothing I can do
I hope you find a together again, strong and loyal enough to forget why
    you even needed to
It's been a long fortnight, and all there's left to do is finish this whiskey
And pray to a god I don't believe in that I'll get drunk enough to believe
    you'll forgive me
My dearest Whitney
Oh, I wish the tables were turned
I didn't know the true depths of what being "together" was
Until we weren't

MANDOLINE

How is any of this true
The way she looks at me so starry-eyed
Dressed in her androgynous suit
No wonder why all my failed loves were guys
The way her hands perfectly cup my cheek
Her precious full lips kiss mine
Her hand on my left knee
Sends shivers down my spine
Before my life was a cobwebbed ghost town
But with just one touch she lit it up in lights
Like we're sweet 16 in high school, every glance from her is electrified
She pulled me into her in the Fall
It took my whole life to take what felt like the first breath of mine
Her hips, oh, her sacred hips, are my altar
Her body, oh, her soft body, is my shrine
I worship this love that's so immortal it's Divine
This is the truest, most definitive meaning of together
Only the prettiest words about her I vocalize
Chest to chest, our hearts beat in perfect time
A rhythm together only we can recognize
And I permanently choose her
The one I was dancing with in my Mary-Janes on the Pier
I looked up at the midnight sapphire sky and saw
These California stars shine just for me and her
It's how she traces hearts all over my scars
She stops all the bleeding
It's how safe together I feel wrapped in her arms
She is all my destiny is needing
It's the love marks she leaves on my collarbone
It's her love that never leaves me naked and alone
It's her warm and sultry heart that I call home
She is the peace I've been searching for
I reach for her like my favorite scarf in the winter
Her soul keeps mine endlessly warm
Every sunrise together is a renewed promise

I wear her arms around my waist like a good luck charm
Her laugh is my favorite love song
Her touch, a lustful melody that lingers
Twisting in the bed sheets we are a Sapphic poem
Swirled verses of desire and perfect rhymes
Her presence is my favorite prose
With every touch, she writes a line
My heart, like pages, flips at every word
Our chemistry is a sonnet etched in her tender grace
And I never saw her coming and I'll never be the same
And this love is brave and it's wild
It's four blue eyes and two twin dancing flames
My heart will always run towards her
Her heart will always take me home
Everywhere and everyone else is nothing more than hollow
See the light of our love in the worst of night-time darkness
Feel the magic in the air when our sparks fly
Hear our connection roar in the silence
Kissing her is what true love tastes like
She is a love story for the ages that's all mine
God is a woman and she knew this perfection would be remembered
Mandoline and I are a love letter to humanity when we're together

THE TWO

RICH RUBIN

Like ships passing in the night they met, the banker and the Kansas boy, and like those ships they went with caution through the hidden locks until they reached the morning and again smooth sailing. That they met is one of those occurrences for which we have no ready explanation, one of those that we call chance: and yet it seems that they had been drifting toward each other for some time, plowing through open sea until they finally converged, at nighttime and alone, in those forbidden–or, heretofore forbidden–places where such meetings happen.

Places in the mind, of course, which directs the meetings of all such groping ships.

The banker: middle-aged, had a wife back in Omaha to think about and a business sense which kept him from indulging in the rash, the untimely, the foolish to which so many others seemed inclined. He was happy, more or less, in the way that people pushing forty-five can settle into something comfortable and unmiserable enough to make it pass for happiness. With the impeccably casual–or was it casually impeccable?–grooming of a man of some importance–that manner which said money even if it never quite said beauty–it was inevitable, he expected, that women would be drawn to him. He was, after all, not ugly, not ugly by any means, and he could, and usually would, be charming, worldly, and arcane. Smooth, very smooth: a diamond which stood out not in the rough, not in that place a diamond can stand out, but among other diamonds, bankers and accountants and attorneys, among whom it seemed–to him–he was somehow in a subtle way set quite distinctively. But he had a wife in Omaha to think about.

The Kansas boy: just that, a boy, and had, then, some of the wildness and the strangely seasoned innocence one has when still a boy. He preferred to say "still a boy" to "only a boy," which seemed somehow like an apology, an admission of inadequacy. He enjoyed, depended on still being a boy, though at twenty he was pushing that boundary. He didn't mind, either, being from Kansas, which he, anyway, thought was the prettiest state in the nation, certainly world enough for him. Between the wheat fields and the thunderstorms at night was all of the excitement that a boy could want. He had never let himself get carried very far. Nebraska once, Missouri in the fall to see the Ozarks in the fall, and even once to Kansas City, which had shocked him and delighted him but which didn't seem like home, like Kansas. Too much noise for one so used to silence, drawn to silence.

Salina, Kansas: nowhere to write home about, a little city–its residents thought: too big, too big already–population around 40,000, known primarily for its flour mill and its grain tanks. There is a Hilton there, and about four miles to the east is an Indian burial pit which the boy used to visit. The Smoky Hill Museum is not too far, and, about twenty miles to the northwest, is Minneapolis–Minneapolis, Kansas–the town the boy was born in.

Like I said, nothing to write home about. But it was here they met, the banker and the Kansas boy, and here the rest of the story–'til the very end–will happen.

It was a Kansas evening, nothing moving but those things the wind moves, and the boy was standing on the corner, watching nothing.

The man was really only going to Abilene, but thought–why not?–the Hilton might be nice, might just be the thing, for one night anyway. He wasn't sure he should have gone on to Salina; it was true that earlier, about exactly on the Kansas and Nebraska border, he had had the strangest feeling, like something wasn't going quite right, like there would be no rooms, like he would have to drive on back to Abilene and stay there in some hotel with a million other bankers. It wasn't that he didn't care for them, that they weren't in their way kind of interesting, but he wanted just to be alone, to drive alone, to see the Kansas sky. To be alone a while.

He ended up, though, at a faceless little "motor inn" a few miles north on the I-70 business loop, in the heart of Salina, what heart there is. It wasn't the Hilton, not the Hilton by any means, but it was good enough, he thought, it had a bed, a desk, and a chair, and that was all he needed for the night. Or so he thought.

The boy stood on the corner of a street in the heart of Salina. Sunday night. The streets of Salina were beginning to see a little action, some people out walking, taking a stroll in the summer air, wrapping up the weekend, finally, like a kind of special gift. The banker breathed deeply, breathed the air he loved so much, and walked briskly.

The Kansas boy, at the corner, smiled. The banker smiled–one of those banker's smiles, so thin-lipped, so mysterious, so little like a smile–and kept walking.

Minutes later he returned, passing the boy again, a second time, and then began to slow, and then stood still–or almost–for what seemed many minutes. *I've got a wife in Omaha to think about* was what ran through his mind those minutes. Yes, ran through, and when it had, was gone, as if to clear

himself, he took a deep, deep breath–what was it he was trying to inhale?–
and casually walked by again. A third time.

The boy watched the people–he knew so few of them these days–and
then the strange man, passing, passing, passing. He smiled.

Hello, the banker said with impeccable casualness.

Hi.

The banker: You're from around here, aren't you?

Yeah, how'd you know?

What could he say? That the boy had eyes the color of the Kansas sky?
That his smile had Kansas sunshine in it? That his overalls against his skin
betrayed him?

I don't know, said the banker, it just seemed... I don't know. I'm from
Omaha. I'm on my way to Abilene. I love your Kansas evenings.

So it went, then, the commonest of meetings, a meeting dictated we
would say at least partly by chance. And yet most special, and the line
between the common and the special can grow thin at times, the two can
start, from their quite separate places, to converge.

They stepped out of the sun, around the corner, into the shade, where
they could talk.

And later, back in the motel...

I just need someone to hold onto, whispered the man. That's not so
bad, is it?

The boy smiled.

His lips grazed the man's cheek, the man's lips–which quivered so little he was sure the boy didn't, couldn't notice)–and with one hand the
man stroked the boy's hair, his back, so slowly, with a touch so sure, so
light, so right, that years later the man could not believe that it had been
his own.

The boy slept well that night; he snored. The banker lay awake most
of the night, tossing a little, thinking of his wife in Omaha, that touch so
light, and listening to the snoring, and the pipes, and sleeping very, very
little on the whole.

It was still a marvel for him, still an exploration, that *his skin could be so
soft!* the man thought, *that angle where his back curves, soft.* He didn't even try
to sleep. And so he saw the clock roll into six o'clock, the boy roll slowly
out of bed, step into his overalls and shoes, splash a little water onto his
face, run his hands briefly through his hair, and grab his cigarettes from
the table, matches from the ashtray, and jacket from the chair.

And the banker saw him leave but did he see him pause for just a moment as he reached the door? He can't remember.

He drove to Abilene that day, arriving just a little early, as was his habit, and it left him just enough time to take a shower, call his wife, and grab a bit of room service before the morning meeting. He doesn't know my name, the banker thought over a tuna sandwich–somehow not quite right at 8 a.m.–he has no idea who I am. He smiled to himself and fixed his tie and combed his hair. And that, he was sure, was that.

And it was, for then. And that's almost all. Except there's this: a young man of twenty-two or so, in a park in Omaha. A man of sixty or so. The older man asks him if he has somewhere to stay in Omaha.

Not really, says the boy, and–smiling now, a smile like Kansas sun–he says, I'm looking for someone.

Well, aren't we all, the older man says. The boy just smiles.

("The Two" appears in Rich Rubin's collection of short stories, *The Day Before It Rained*. www.richrubinwriter.com)

WHAT KIND OF ROMANTIC ARE YOU?

JAN STECKEL

RICHARD

When you pray, Ty, do you pray as a way to commune with God? Do you pray for strength? Do you pray for enlightenment? Does it come when you pray for it? Or do you sometimes feel you're pitching rocks down a well so deep you'll never hear a splash?

Pass the pickles. I told you this place had the best corned beef. I didn't know Monique was working here now, though. Hey, Monique, would you bring us some mustard the next time around?

Love that skirt.

It seemed blasphemous to me when the Giants got down on their knees and prayed for the winning field goal against the Forty-Niners in the play-offs. I tried to imagine what they could be saying. "Heavenly Father, send me to the Super Bowl. Nevertheless, not as I will, but as Thou wilt." When that football sailed through the goal posts, I squinted hard, but I could not see the hand of God in it. If God didn't answer the prayers of my grandmother's cousins to save their babies from the gas chamber, why should He listen to a linebacker? Because the linebacker is addressing Jesus instead of Yahweh? I can't believe that God would ignore the prayers of the Jewesses simply because they didn't go through proper channels.

Thanks, Monique. You're a doll.

(Can you believe all that hokey stuff about moving to New York and waitressing while she writes? What does she write, True Confessions? Maybe how she and Nick made love in the elevator between floors to show their joie de vivre. Or about the time Sean's dad came after her dad with a pistol because she got his little boy in trouble.)

So, Ty, do you attribute the good in the world to God and the evil in it to man? Will you say I am arrogant to suppose we could understand God's plan? That God the watchmaker made the machine, and now He's leaning back and observing it run? That for Him to intervene to save us from our own choices would nullify our status as moral beings?

His non-interventionism is relatively recent. Why did God save Daniel from the mouth of the lion and not Yaakov from the hands of the S.S.? My father says God paid less attention to the prayers of the Jews after the birth of Christ not because Jesus was the Messiah, but because the spread of Christianity led to an unmanageable increase in the volume of prayers addressed to the Occupant of the Throne of Heaven. This created such a bureaucratic backlog that God didn't actually hear about the

Holocaust until 1955. When He discovered what had happened, there was hell to pay in Heaven, but it was too late to rectify the oversight.

TYLER

My faith is an emotional response. I'd like to play you the Pergolesi *Magnificat*, because it reaches toward heaven and the mind of God.

RICHARD

Hey, Monique, we're ready for the check.

TYLER

In high school I was in love with a girl named Lauren. She had long black hair that she used to fasten into a ponytail with an elastic tie that had a little gold ball on it. I would sit behind her in class staring with great longing and affection at that little gold ball. One day I asked her to a movie, and–to my shock–she said yes. After the movie, we sat on a bus-stop bench, and I kissed her for hours. I asked her to a lot of stupid movies so we could kiss on the bus-stop bench. One night, she sneaked out of her house and walked to mine. She tapped on the window; I removed the screen, and she climbed in. We took off our clothes and lay in my bed kissing and caressing each other. She told me how beautiful my body was, and I told her how much I loved her. After several hours of this, she told me she wanted me. I asked her if she loved me. She admitted she did not, but that she loved my blue eyes and my blond hair and my strong hands. I asked her to wait. She said she had no more patience. She got up and got dressed and left in anger, and she never returned or went out with me again.

RICHARD

Before I made love to Gabriela, she didn't love me; she was just a groupie. She had the hots for me after my band played at a party at one of her friend's houses. I drove her out to an abandoned construction site and made love to her on the hood of the Galaxie. After several heart-stopping orgasms, she discovered she was in love with me.

GABRIELA

What is it in the voice of a man that goes straight to your heart before your mind can make any defense? I liked his thick brown hair that fell in curls around his neck, the way he moved, and the expressions of his face when he sang. It was none of these, however, nor any of the things that Richard said, but the tone of voice in which he said them, that made me love him. At the party in Malibu, he wore a black T-shirt and jeans. I had on my red dress. We met in the kitchen after the second set. He was soaked with sweat, and his cheeks were flushed. He asked if I wanted to go for a drive. Six weeks later I moved into the place he shared with you, Ty.

TYLER

The first time I saw Richard, he was kneeling over a man stretched out on the cement in front of a sidewalk cafe. He was asking the people around to help move the man out of the sun, but no one wanted to touch him. They said, we know this guy. He's been like this before. It's best not to get involved.

I said, I'll help. I took the man's shoulders and Richard took his legs, and we moved him onto the grass under a tree. One of the man's forearms was darker than the other; it looked dead. The hand was bent into a claw. When we set him down, he moaned and reached out that hand, palm up, toward Richard, who took it in his own without hesitation and asked me to go call 911.

When I came back Richard was still holding the man's hand, and the man was speaking to him urgently and unintelligibly. Richard kept saying, I'm sorry, I can't understand you. The paramedics are coming. It'll be all right. I'm sorry, I can't understand you.

After the ambulance left with the man, Richard sat on the grass glaring at the people in the café for a few minutes. Then he seemed to remember that I was there. He looked at me, and all the anger went out of his face. Let's go somewhere else, he said. We were both sixteen.

I guess the only person I care more about than Richard is my brother, but it's a different kind of caring. Once when we were kids, Christopher and I went on a hike in the woods with a couple of boys my age. We ran out of water early, it was hard for Christopher to keep up, and in the late afternoon we walked into a beehive. We were in a ravine, and the only way to get away from the cloud of bees was to run through it. I grabbed Christopher's hand and told him to run, but he wouldn't move. One of the boys started to scream as the bees began stinging him. I pulled Christopher's arm roughly and shouted at him, and he let me yank him into motion. As we ran the air seemed dark with the bees and angry with

119

their buzzing, and the one boy's screaming turned to a barely human yelp-
ing. I made my little brother run through the bees and for many yards
beyond, until the forest was silent again. That boy had to spend the night
in the hospital, and I was stung on the eyelid and my eye swelled shut, but
Christopher didn't get stung at all.

I don't feel protective of Richard.

RICHARD

I can't really believe in God, Gabriela, but sometimes I walk into the
church on Ocean Avenue and stand in the back watching all the votive
candles burn. It makes me happy to see how much faith there is in the
world, even though I don't have it myself. That's how I feel when I look at
Tyler. He seems made of thin alabaster, and his unquestioning love of God
illuminates him from within. I try to do the right thing, but Tyler doesn't
have to try. His goodness comes to him naturally.

TYLER

Richard is practicing with the band at the house in Venice. Gabriela
and I go down to the beach to swim. Her black bathing suit is scooped
low in back, showing skin that is smooth and white. As she ties her hair
back, I see the muscles in her shoulders move under that smooth skin, and
I have to look away. She runs straight into the water and dives under a
wave without taking any time to get used to the cold. I follow and dare
her to swim out to a distant buoy with me. She makes it out to the buoy,
but then she is tired and afraid to start back for the beach. I tell her to hold
onto my shoulders. Her hands are cool and soft. As I swim slowly toward
the shore, her small breasts brush against my back. I feel guilty that I
tempted her to swim too far, but not sorry.

GABRIELA

Tyler and I are dancing to Richard's music in the club. My arms and
feet move fluidly, and my body moves with them. Ty thinks of his spirit as
being trapped within his flesh. I feel strongly that I am my body, not that
I inhabit it. We have a good table near the front. Chris and Monique's
chairs are empty. No doubt they're out necking in the parking lot. I should
show Chris how to open a matchbook and light a match using just his left
hand. It's good practice for unhooking bras, which I believe is still beyond

him. Tyler looks unhappy. He's afraid Monique is going to eat his little brother up alive. Richard sings a *Cuatro Cuarenta* song I taught him; his accent is not too bad.

RICHARD
Saliendo del Conde un día la vi,
vestida de rojo como maniquí,
su cuerpo el centro de toda atención,
de toda la calle, de todo varón....

...Yo no se lo que me pasa a mí,
pero yo me siento solo.
Por eso ahora, ya yo no volveré a querer.

GABRIELA
When I was sixteen, I got a fake ID, and I finally let an older friend of mine get me up in one of my brothers' clothes and take me out dancing. The brief appeal of looking like a boy; I told myself it was only one more form of narcissism. But I was struck by how it felt when the woman tied my tie for me and let the backs of her hands brush against my breast. Looking down at her bent head, at her small-boned wrists, I felt an unfamiliar protectiveness stir inside me. I lifted her face in my hands, and I kissed her. We went to a gay disco in Hollywood and danced all night. The women pretended to be tough or femmes fatales; the men danced exuberantly. I felt, momentarily, as though I had come home.

TYLER
The guitar and bass are out of tune with each other again. Richard's voice has a rough charisma and a heartbreaking strain when tender. He is not necessarily always on key. I am glad I don't have absolute pitch. Hell must be a waiting room where you sit forever while in the next room a soprano practices her scales slightly flat. What do the words in the song mean?

GABRIELA
Leaving the Conde one day I saw her,
dressed in red like a mannequin,
her body the center of all attention,

of the whole street, of all the young men....

...I don't know what's happening to me,
but I feel lonely.
That's why now, I won't love again.

GABRIELA

I am lying on the long living room couch, my head touching Tyler's thigh, with my legs draped over Richard's lap. I look up at you and offer you the joint, Ty, out of mere politeness, knowing you will courteously refuse. Oh well, when the trumpet blows, judgment will find you with clean hands and a pure heart, wishing you had sinned a little.

Ty, you look as though you were painted on the ceiling. Were you given the face of an androgynous angel as evidence of the existence of an artistic God? You are beautiful, but you appear too serene to invite the approaches of women, who find the immobile symmetry of your face forbidding. When the band plays you are strangely still in the midst of a rocking crowd, as though what moved the rest of us could not move you. You look like a carving of yourself recumbent on your own tomb. You need to be reminded that perfection of execution is inhuman. You need something to disarrange your hair and clothes and give you an expression of anxiousness and yearning.

RICHARD

Ty is not like us romantics: phoenix and ashes, passion and heartbreak, then ready for passion again. He is like still cool water, that can't be set afire.

TYLER

I leave them and go to my room. I put *Carmina Burana* on the stereo, and I lie back on my bed.

Stetit puella
rufa tunica;
si quis eam tetigit
tunica crepuit.
Eia, eia.

There stood a young girl
in a red tunic;
if anyone touched her,
the tunic rustled.
Heigho, heigho.

TYLER

I have to keep lighting the pilot light of the oven because Richard and Gabriela don't smell gas. The whole apartment would fill with gas before they would know. I can't get them to check the pilot. If I leave for a weekend, will they blow themselves up?

RICHARD

Monique of the stretch-knit miniskirt and henna-ed hair: when you enter a room you smile at all the men and don't even notice the women. How did I get here in your little girl's bedroom, with the icons of the saints next to the plastic horses on your shelves, as if you had not had your second abortion before you dropped out of high school? The fashion magazine on the vanity table is open to this quiz:

What Kind of Romantic Are You?
Incurable, passionate or contemporary?
Take this quiz to find out what your romantic style is.

1. A man you've had your eye on finally asks you to dinner. On your first date you wear:
a. A leather mini-skirt.
b. Silk pants and a shirt.
c. A sensational red dress.

2. You would find it incredibly romantic, if your man were to:
a. Kiss the inside of your wrists.
b. Give you a single, handpicked flower.
c. Leave you a sexy message on your answering machine.

3. The predominant colors in your wardrobe are:
a. Soft pastels.
b. Vibrant, vivid brights.
c. Black, white and neutrals.

SCORING Add up your points below, and discover what kind of a
romantic you are:

1. a-3 b-1 c-2
2. a-3 b-2 c-1
3. a-2 b-3 c-1

(1-3) A Contemporary Romantic
(4-6) A True Romantic
(7-9) A Passionate Romantic

   The saints regard me gravely, as though you are a virgin I am about to
deflower. *Un libstu mikh mit varer libe, to kum tsu mir, mayn guter shats.* If you
love me with true love, come to me, my beloved...

GABRIELA
Driving late at night on curving unlit roads in the Ventura Hills... the
big American car–1970 maroon Buick Skylark, automatic on the column–
has such a wide turning radius, makes it a challenge, but the 350 V-8
engine gives you pick-up and power to make up for the thing being such
a whale. A small gray fox freezes in the headlights. We stare at each other,
the fox's eyes reflecting back red. Where is Richard so late at night?

TYLER
When I open the front door I startle Gabriela in the living room. She
is wearing only an over-sized white T-shirt. Her black hair spills around
her shoulders. Her legs are long and smooth. The place smells like gas. She
asks me if Richard is carrying on with Monique. I betray Richard pas-
sively by my silence. She goes to bed, and I light the pilot light in the oven.
In my bedroom I put the Mozart *Requiem* on the stereo and lie down. Most
nights I imagine I am Gabriela being made love to by Richard. Tonight, I
imagine how I would feel if Richard made love to me.

Lacrimosa dies illa,
qua resurget ex favilla
judicandus homo reus.
Huic ergo parce, Deus...

That day is one of weeping,
on which shall rise again from the ashes
the guilty man, to be judged.
Therefore, spare this one, O God.

GABRIELA
I am walking alone at Trancas. The beach is destitute now of its bean clams and sand crabs, kelp holdfasts and jellyfish, dogs' footprints and the scratches of sandpipers' feet. The wind comes across off the water with nothing to stop it. The tide has drained away and left isolate pools on the shore. So gray and white, this empty beach...

RICHARD
Like the Boss sings, Gabriela:
"Everything dies baby that's a fact,
but maybe everything that dies someday comes back.
Put your makeup on, fix your hair up pretty,
and meet me tonight in Atlantic City..."

GABRIELA
Back in my parents' house, having left Richard, I dream of a man pierced by the spokes of a gyroscope, like the man impaled on the harp strings in the Hieronymus Bosch painting. The man in my dream is blond; his eyes are blue. It is Tyler, transfixed on the spokes of a wheel within a wheel, and as it turns and turns his face remains serene.

RICHARD
Ah, you never loved me. If you'd loved me, you'd have stayed.

TYLER
I think of Gabriela in all her unsubtlety, with her brass earrings and her tacky Latin whorehouse music, trying to draw me out about my sex-

uality. I should have asked her, Why do you think God made everyone else in your image? I should have said, You don't know me.

RICHARD
Ty is a choirboy.

TYLER
I see pictures on the news of an oil spill on a lake, and the lake is burning.

RICHARD
Ty is an old woman.

TYLER
Christopher calls me on the phone, "Tyler, help me, I'm scared, help me." He is at Monique's. I go there and find my brother freaking out while Richard and Monique are too absorbed in each other to do anything about it. Richard got LSD somewhere, and they have all taken some. Christopher is crying, and when I touch him, he starts screaming and tries to punch me. I have to wrestle him to the ground, like our childhood when he used to fly at me flailing wildly and my only job was to grab his wrists to keep his fists away from my face. I hold him and comfort him, until at last I get him quiet.

I yell at Richard and Monique for taking acid without leaving one person in possession of his wits the way you're supposed to. Richard says, "It's not my fault if Chris can't tell what's real and what isn't." I hit him in the mouth, knocking him back against the wall. Christopher starts screaming again. Richard spits blood and grins sourly. "Take your baby brother home, Ty."

For two days Richard and I avoid each other in our big apartment. Late the second night I hear a crash from his room.

RICHARD
I am staring at my reflection in the bedroom window. I see the eyes that burned for her, and before I understand what I'm doing my hand has gone through the window and blood is dripping from my wrist. Ty bursts in and looks frightened as I tell him my heart is ashes, I'm sorry about the carpet, I'm sorry about the window. He binds my hand with a T-shirt and

tries to make me hold it above my head, but I tell him I'm so full of ashes I can taste them in my mouth. I can't sing anymore, my throat is so dry, and all the fire that burned in me has gone out.

TYLER

I drive him to the emergency room where they pick all the bits of glass out of his hand. He thinks it will take him a thousand years to rise from these ashes, but it will only take him a few months.

About the Authors

K.S. Trenten

K.S. Trenten lives in the South Bay area with her husband, two cats, and a crowd of characters in her head; all shouting for attention. Follow K.S. Trenten, locate her published works, or read free samples at...

Facebook
http://www://facebook.com/rhodrymavelyne/

Twitter
https://twitter.com/rhodrymavelyne

Goodreads
https://www.goodreads.com/author/show/14876500.K_S_Trenten

Amazon Author Page
http://www.amazon.com/author/kstrenten

Nine Star Press Author Page
https://ninestarpress.com/authors/k-s-trenten/

The Cauldron of Eternal Inspiration
http://www://inspirationcauldron.wordpress.com

Pat Henshaw

Pat Henshaw has led an interesting life starting as a theatrical costumer, then moving to newspaper editor, arts reviewer, and book columnist. In addition to newspapers, she worked as a publicist and an English composition instructor. Her most challenging roles have been as a wife, a mother to two brilliant daughters, and grandma to twins.

Although she was born in Nebraska, she has lived on all three U.S. coasts: in Texas, in Northern Virginia, and in California. She has also traveled extensively around the world, on a trip down the Nile, riding an elephant in Thailand, and touring Europe. After she retired, she fulfilled a lifelong dream to become an author. Through all her life experiences, she still maintains: *Every day is a good day for romance.*

R.L. MERRILL

R.L. Merrill brings you stories of Hope, Love, and Rock 'n' Roll featuring quirky and relatable characters. Whether she's writing contemporary, paranormal, or supernatural, she loves to give readers a shiver with compelling stories that will stay with you long after. You can find her connecting with readers on social media, advocating for America's youth, raising two brilliant teenagers, writing horror-infused music reviews for HorrorAddicts.net, trying desperately to get that back piece finished in the tattoo chair, or headbanging at a rock show near her home in the San Francisco Bay Area! Stay tuned for more Rock 'n' Romance.

LIZ FARAIM

Liz Fariam has a full plate between balancing a day job, parenting, writing, and finding some semblance of a social life. In past lives, she has been a soldier, a bartender, a shoe salesperson, an assistant museum curator, and even a driving instructor. She focuses her writing on strong, queer, female leads who don't back down. Liz transplanted to California from New York over thirty years ago, and now lives in the East Bay Area. She enjoys exploring nature with her wife and son.

RICHARD MAY

Richard May writes Gay fiction. His work has appeared in numerous literary journals, story anthologies, and his story collections *Ginger Snaps: Photos & Stories of Redheaded Queer People*, *Inhuman Beings*, *Because of Roses*, and *Gay All Year*. He is a member of the 18th Street Writers and the Bay Area Queer Writers Association. Rick organizes the LGBTQ book club for Alibi Bookshop in Vallejo, California. He lives in the North Bay.

VINCENT TRAUGHBER MEIS

Vincent Traughber Meis worked for many years as an English as a Second Language (ESL) teacher in the San Francisco Bay Area, Spain, Saudi Arabia and Mexico, publishing many academic articles in his field. He published travel articles, poems, and book reviews in publications such as, *The Advocate*, *LA Weekly*, *In Style*, and *Our World* in the 1980s and 1990s. Eight of his nine published novels are set at least partially in foreign countries, and his book of short stories focuses on countries around the world. Several of his novels have won Rainbow Awards and two of his novels, including *First Born Sons*, were awarded Reader Views Silver Awards. He has published short stories in a number of collections and has achieved Finalist status in a few short fiction contests. He lives in San Leandro, California and Puerto Vallarta, Mexico.

M.D. NEU

Growing up in an accepting family author M.D. Neu always wondered why there were never stories reflecting our diverse queer society. Surrounded by characters that only mirrored heterosexual society, he decided to change that and began writing, wanting to tell epic stories that reflect our varied world. Over the years, Neu has written several Urban Fantasy, Science Fiction, and Paranormal works. His Science Fiction novels *A New World-Contact* and *Conviction* won the 2018-2019 International Rainbow Awards: Best Gay Alternative Universe/Reality & Sci-Fi / Futuristic books. Recently, his novella *T.A.D.-The Angel of Death* won the 2020-2021 International Rainbow Awards: Best Gay Alternative Universe/Reality and was one of the Runner Ups for Best Gay Book. Neu's debut novel, *The Calling*, was featured in the *San Jose Mercury News* (January 2018) garnering him national recognition. When not writing M.D. Neu works for a non-profit in Silicon Valley and travels with his husband of twenty-plus years.

Wayne Goodman

Wayne Goodman has lived in the San Francisco Bay Area most of his life (with too many cats). Goodman hosts Queer Words Podcast, conversations with queer-identified authors about their works and lives. When not writing or recording, he enjoys playing Gilded Age parlor music on the piano, with an emphasis on women, gay, and Black composers.

Michael Alenyikov

Michael Alenyikov is the author of *Ivan and Misha* (Northwestern University Press), which won the Northern California Book Award for Fiction and was a Finalist for the Edmund White Award for Debut Fiction. His second book, *Sorrow's Drive*, was published in 2022 (Spectrum Books). His writing has appeared in: *The Georgia Review, Foglifter, Chicago Quarterly Review, James White Review, Catamaran Literary Reader*, and many other publications. Two short stories were nominated for the Pushcart Prize. His story, "Arithmetic," was performed on stage by San Francisco's acclaimed Word for Word acting company. Three have appeared in the anthology series, *Best Gay Stories* (Lethe Press). A New York City native and longtime resident of San Francisco, he's a former clinical psychologist, long disabled with ME/CFS.

Sarah White

Hanging out in her thirties, Sarah is a bisexual, born and raised Bay Area native. Sarah writes queer culture and queer historical articles for a national LGBTQ magazine, is an LGBTQ activist, and a youth crisis counselor for the Trevor Project. "Liking the wine and not the label" (*Schitt's Creek* reference) is Sarah's favorite part of being bisexual because she is living proof that love and attraction is not binary, it is continuous, untamed, and pure. Sarah writes her poetry based on her real life experiences of thriving and failing at love as a bisexual woman in the 21st Century. Sarah would like to thank BAQWA for this humbling opportunity to showcase her writing and provide a platform to connect with other queer people leaving their rainbow mark on the world by just breathing in and breathing out their truth.

RICH RUBIN

Rich Rubin has written fiction for decades. He also spent thirty years writing about travel and food (the best job in the world, literally), with over 1000 stories in print. He produced Philadelphia's GayFest! Festival of LGBTQ+ theater for six years, and his work as playwright and director has been seen in New York, Philadelphia, Seattle, and San Francisco. He lives in Sonoma County, California. You can find out more at www.richrubinwriter.com.

JAN STECKEL

Jan Steckel's debut fiction collection *Ghosts and Oceans* came out from Zeitgeist Press in 2023. Her poetry book *The Horizontal Poet* (Zeitgeist Press, 2011) won a 2012 Lambda Literary Award. Her poetry book *Like Flesh Covers Bone* (Zeitgeist Press, 2018) won two Rainbow Awards. Her fiction chapbook *Mixing Tracks* (Gertrude Press, 2009) and poetry chapbook *The Underwater Hospital* (Zeitgeist Press, 2006) also won awards. Her creative prose and poetry have appeared in *Scholastic Magazine*, *Yale Medicine*, *Bellevue Literary Review*, *Canary*, *Assaracus* and elsewhere. She lives in Oakland, California.

All proceeds from this limited-time anthology will be donated to Solano Pride Center.

Printed in the USA
CPSIA information can be obtained
at www.ICGtesting.com
LVHW021824190924
791567LV00010B/232